WHISTLING PAST THE VEIL

Whistling Past the Veil

A Collection of Stories All Knocking On Death's Door

by

A. ELIZABETH HERTING

Adelaide Books
New York / Lisbon
2019

WHISTLING PAST THE VEIL
A Collection of Stories All Knocking On Death's Door
By A. Elizabeth Herting

Published by Adelaide Books, New York / Lisbon
adelaidebooks.org
Editor-in-Chief
Stevan V. Nikolic

For any information, please address Adelaide Books
at info@adelaidebooks.org
or write to:
Adelaide Books
244 Fifth Ave. Suite D27
New York, NY, 10001

ISBN-10: 1-949180-94-8
ISBN-13: 978-1-949180-94-7

Printed in the United States of America

To Chuck, Joan Claire, Elizabeth and Charlie,

My Life, My Loves...

Thank you for the inspiration...

Contents

Chrysalis

There is nothing poetic in death.

Death is painful, degrading and filled with shit and bodily fluids and torment.

Claudia Cooper had been witness to endless days of suffering. It had been almost two weeks and yet her father lingered on. What on earth was he waiting for? The hospital called her when he was admitted, her name being the only one he'd listed. She hadn't spoken to him in well over six months. Now here she was by his side, the only witness to his final, heartbreaking days.

Claudia and her father never enjoyed a typical loving relationship. He'd went away when she was six-years old, leaving her with years of abandonment issues and phobias. At least that's what the non-stop, psychobabble, parade of her therapist's greatest hits mentally spat out to her daily. Her mother, Claire, went on an eternal quest to "find herself" after her father left, whatever the hell that meant. The only thing it meant to Claudia was being dragged by her from one shrink's office to the next. The entirety of her childhood spent examining every nook and cranny of her mind when the only thing she wanted to do was escape in a great, dramatic flourish. Exactly like her father.

What are your emotions, Claudia? On a scale from one to ten, can you describe your level of anger? Tell me, Claudia, about the day your father left you...

"Enough!" she said to the sleeping, shrunken man in the bed, her voice reverberating around the dingy old hospital room. The only thing the crew of psychotherapists and all the other "ists" in her life needed to know was she yearned to be free. Free from being forced to endure anymore mental prodding. She detected the stifling, soul-crushing looks of concern were a facade to mask professional indifference. They had no stake in her, not really. They were being paid handsomely to nod sagely, asking her the same questions in ten different ways and angles. She had tried throughout the years to explain it to them but with very limited success. None of them ever believed that she didn't hate him for leaving, not at all. She was consumed with envy that he had escaped.

She jumped up from her chair as he moaned in pain, the only real response she'd seen from him in over an hour. The hospice worker had been in earlier, keeping him hopped up on morphine and ativan for anxiety. *Apparently, dying causes anxiety. Who knew?* Claudia tried to swallow her bitterness as she watched him struggle in his manufactured sleep. *If this is how we check out, I hope to get hit by a bus or jump off of a cliff. Anything but this agonizing slog into eternity, or total nothingness.* Claudia didn't know which she would choose, preferred not to think of it. Every breath seemed a chore for him, his suffering excruciating as his body waged war against itself in a feeble effort to slow down the inevitable.

Her mother had bounced in earlier that morning on her way to her latest meditation ceremony. What rot. Claire's penchant for chasing shadows instead of acknowledging her own breathing daughter left Claudia no other option than to become the adult, the years adding to the wall of resentment between them. Claire leaping from one situation to the next without any care of the consequences was maddening. Claudia felt each burden in her mother's stead, weighted down with them. Her mother emerged time and time again from her chrysalis, an exquisite butterfly floating away to her next adventure. Claudia had been abandoned, more of a moth than a butterfly if she was being honest. Both of her parents had followed their own paths away from her, always away.

Her father fancied himself an actor. He spent years trodding the boards of every second-rate, dinner theater stage and off-off Broadway production. Broadway, but only if you were referring to Broadway street in south Toledo, Ohio. She remembered that his biggest credit was as "Man #2" in an episode of "Friends" many years back. She had recorded it on their old VCR, rewinding his brief scene over and over as a child, trying to reach out to him through the television screen.

He would land the occasional acting job here and there but to him, it really didn't matter much. As long as he could scrape by, it allowed him to follow his real passion. The only vivid memories she had of him were of his booming voice. The dramatic pauses and expressions he used while reciting the only lines that ever held any real meaning for him. She always wondered at their potency, the ability of written words from centuries ago to possess and enthrall her father, making him wander the back streets, festivals and theaters in search of them. No—Claudia and her mother only ever had one true rival, a man who died in 1616. William Shakespeare.

Karen, her father's main nurse, came in to check his vitals, moving through the room with practiced speed. Claudia really liked Karen, her blunt speaking style and dry sense of humor striking a familiar chord with her. They'd gotten to know each other well and became fast friends. Claudia knew she needed one honest person in her life, especially now that her father was nearing the end.

Even as her father whittled away into decrepitude, he was still quite the charmer. The golf ball sized tumor in his head had mixed up enough of his wiring so that he could only recite Shakespeare quotes. This fascinated the hospital staff, especially Karen, who referred to him as "the Bard." Claudia actually thought it was fitting. She could see the pleasure in her father's eyes each time Karen came in, could tell he was still trying to flirt with her even in his final days, the old bastard.

"Hiya kid, how's the Bard holding up today?" Karen asked, briefly squeezing Claudia on the shoulder on her way to the bed. Claudia noticed that Karen was constantly in motion; she didn't think she had ever seen the nurse stay in one place for more than a minute.

"Not bad, about the same I guess. Earlier he woke up and said '*I burn, I pine, I perish!*' I tried to find it in the book, think it was from either '*Lear*' or '*the Shrew,*'" Claudia said sardonically. She purchased an enormous bible of Shakespeare's works in an effort to understand what her father was saying. The strangeness of the tumor caused him to string together random lines from the famous playwright to tell them what he needed. It had become a game, trying to pull out his meaning from the archaic writing. Claudia begrudgingly admired the poetry of the words, finding a spark of the passion that had ignited her father's life-long obsession. Claudia didn't want to admire Shakespeare, wanted to hate him. Her latest shrink would say she partially blamed him for her father's absence, as irrational as that was. After a while, Shakespeare's words grew on her, Claudia puzzling out each phrase as her father attempted to communicate. It seemed she was her father's daughter after all.

The Bard, sensing his favorite nurse had entered the room, opened his eyes. They were clouded by drugs and sleep, yet still brimming with a spark of his old mischief. Claudia felt a tug at her heart, still loving him a little in spite of it all.

"*Doubt thou the stars are fire, Doubt that the sun doth move. Doubt truth to be a liar, But never doubt I love,*" he intoned, a trace of his rich baritone still breaking through as he recited the well-loved words.

"Oh, wait a sec...let me look, I believe that line is from…"

"Hamlet," Karen said, holding his hand gently. "And I'm rather fond of you too, you old goat, although I am sure you say that to all the girls."

Claudia looked up in surprise at the nurse, finding a trace of tenderness there. She knew that Karen was recently divorced, in her mid-fifties, still lithe and pretty. If circumstances were different, she knew the Bard would pursue the relationship, age difference be damned. He was an unabashed ladies' man; it went with the territory. As it was, the only date he had to look forward to was quickly approaching. Like the "*ides of March,*" as Shakespeare would say, for her father would never live to see his seventy-first birthday.

"I know how to do my research," Karen said cheerfully to him, "especially where my number one patient is concerned." She took a damp cloth to his forehead, smoothing back the wisps of receding hair, propping him up with one arm and quickly fluffing up the pillows underneath.

"For a quart of ale is a meal for a king..." he sputtered out, a jagged cough cutting off the last word.

"I'm sorry Bard, we're not serving ale today, but I will get you some fresh ice chips." Karen took a small plastic spoon from the nightstand and carefully wet his lips with the ice she'd brought, the Bard looking up at her gratefully. Ice was the only thing he could tolerate these days, any kind of food caused immediate vomiting. The hospice nurse told them that at this stage in the dying process, feeding the patient was actually cruel. The Bard hadn't had a real meal in over a week.

Satisfied that his thirst was quenched, he leaned back onto the pillow and fell into an uneasy slumber. Karen pulled the blanket up around his frail body, tucking him in like a small boy and turned off the light above his bed. Dusk was seeping in through the only window in the room, giving the objects within an unearthly glow. Karen approached Claudia, looking at her with a critical eye.

"Kid, I hate to tell you this, but you look like shit. You need sleep, a hot shower and a decent meal. The Bard's not going anywhere. Why don't you go home and freshen up? My shift's over. I'll sit with him awhile"

Tears sprang to Claudia's eyes. She shared her father's affection for the kind lady. Claudia never realized how much she craved what Karen offered freely: maternal concern. How her shrink would love to analyze that!

"Thanks K, I don't want to go all the way home. Maybe I'll just jump in the shower down the hall and try to eat one of those cardboard sandwiches in the cafeteria. That should do the trick."

Karen pulled up a plastic chair, settling in right next to her father's bed. "Well, if that's the best I can get from you, I'll take it. The Bard is lucky to have you, Claudie," she whispered, using Claudia's childhood name. Claudia smiled, she had told Karen about her nickname, enjoyed hearing it from her. "I am sure that he knows it."

Claudia nodded, quickly turning away so that Karen wouldn't see the tears escaping. She crept out of the room as Karen held her father's hand. The picture of the two bathed in the dying light would be forever imprinted onto her mind. Regret coursing through her, she closed the door and went off in search of sustenance.

Before leaving town, her father would visit her occasionally. He never stayed in one place long, finding a new company or theater after every production. Sometimes, the infrequent child support checks would include a card or playbill from his latest show. Claire, constantly complaining about their financial situation, railed against him at every opportunity. Claudia could understand her mother's frustration, her father was impossible to pin down.

When her parents first met, they were young and part of the same acting company. Claire had fallen hard for the brilliant young actor during "A Midsummer's Night Dream," sighing over his jaunty, mischievous Puck as she danced around him, an expendable extra, trying very hard to be noticed. Claudia was living proof that he noticed. They married within two months of meeting. Claudia was brought into their idyllic existence as the living embodiment of their bond, his enchanting mother eclipsing all others in her father's eyes. All others except for the great playwright himself, his tantalizing words reaching out through the centuries to snatch him away from them.

There was never any doubt that he was the better actor, his raw talent and masterful delivery making him an instant hit wherever they went. They lived like gypsies at first, his parents traveling from theater to theater, going where the acting jobs led them. He played every role, in every possible combination and part. All of the heroes and villains, all of the bravado and drama and tragedy, all of it lived within him. Her mother grew resentful, hating the way he threw himself into his work, even at the expense of his little family. They grew farther apart as he stayed at the theater late into the night, eventually finding excuses not to come home at all.

He would try to speak to Claudia directly, but Claire would intercept all correspondence throughout the years as they tried to drown their sorrows in endless psychoanalysis. From time to time, she would hear word of him, a review here and there online or a snippet of her mother's angered conversations. Fascinated by the thought of him standing on stage, she imagined him thrilling an audience with the sheer force of his presence. Claudia had tried taking drama classes in school, but never felt any passion for it. She was awful, if she was being honest with herself, finding more poetry in science and math. She became the left brain to her parents' right half, preferring logic to magic and wispy dreams.

When she was a junior in high school, her father's latest company rolled into town to put on a production of "Othello" at the run down theater downtown. Claire was away at some new age therapy convention out of state, leaving her daughter to her own devices. Rebellion wasn't Claudia's style, but she decided that this would be her only chance to see him. He was surprised and excited to hear from her, eagerly agreeing to a meeting. They were to meet at a coffee shop right next to the theater after his matinee performance. Claudia called herself in sick to school that day. She'd been able to pull it off, calling the school for years—apparently she was quite a fine actress when impersonating her own mother on the school's attendance line. She bought a ticket to the show and sat as far back as she dared, defiantly daring her father to impress her.

The instant he entered, her heart sank. Without wanting to, she became utterly engrossed by his performance, so raw and emotional. The flowery language sounded foreign to her modern ears, but his delivery of the lines did not. She could hear in their impact, an explanation for his desertion, a reasoning behind it. Ration and logic were turned on their head as she watched her father up there in the dark. All the love she craved from him living and breathing in his rage-filled Othello.

She ran out at the end, right past the coffee house and out of his life for the next five years, refusing all contact with him. It wasn't until she was in her twenties that she relented, her father calling and emailing the second she moved away from her mother's house. She never told him why she stood him up that day, could never bear to think of it.

Claudia reached the cafeteria lost in her memories. All the time they had lost, so many years of missed opportunities. Only now, when it was too late, did she have a chance to know him. When the hour of his death was on hand.

Five-year-old Claudie swings high into the air gasping with joy, her handsome Daddy lifting her higher and higher until she can feel the hot stage lights on her upturned face. He is young, the most handsome Daddy in the whole wide world with his head full of jet-black hair and bright green eyes. Eyes that are the same shade as Claudie's, everyone always says so. No one in her afternoon kindie class has a Daddy like hers, especially one who dresses up for a living-just like a superhero! Daddy places her gently on the stage, just behind the curtain and gives her a special wink. His eyes are rimmed with black stage makeup, deep and expressive. He strides out onto the stage; the audience applauding in appreciation at the mere sight of him. Claudie watches, completely mesmerized as he says the words she has seen him practice over a million times in the mirror at home.

"*But soft! What light through yonder window breaks? It is the east and Juliet is the sun...*"

"*Arise fair sun, and kill the envious moon!*" the Bard's commanding voice reached out across the room, carrying an echo of its former glory. It jolted Claudia out of her childhood memory, sending her sprawling from the chair and forcing her back into the present with its intensity. *I fell asleep in the chair again. Damn it! What if he needed me?* She scrambled to her feet, wiping the sleep from her eyes and looked at him in complete astonishment.

He was halfway sitting up, as much as he possibly could in his weakened state, his gaze bright and intelligent. She sucked in her breath as he took a deep breath and continued addressing her in a firm voice, a tone she never thought to hear from him again.

"*O! Let me not be mad, not mad, sweet heaven; keep me in temper; I would not be mad!*"

"Hang on Dad," she said cautiously, searching in vain for the overturned book. She wasn't sure if she looked for the book out of fear or necessity, but she understood the tone of his words well enough without it. She was still trying to wake up, having slept soundly for over three hours since returning from the cafeteria. This was the most cognizant and aware she had seen him in weeks, an incredible, miraculous development. She thought of trying to page Karen but didn't want to lose the moment, whatever the hell this was.

"*Like as the waves make towards the pebbl'd shore, so do our minutes, hasten to their end,*" he said, trying to reach out to her, make his meaning clear.

"Dad, let me know how to help you, how to make you comfortable, I know this is hard."

"*End!*" he said in a raised voice, "*We are time's subjects, and time bids be gone!*"

Claudia gaped at him, surprised and groped for the chair next to his bed. She thought back to the conversation she'd had with Karen days ago, that sometimes terminal patients rallied just before the end. Was that what this was? Or was there any chance, no matter how small, that he was somehow improving? *Goddamnit, Karen, why aren't you here? I need you now!*

His voice lowered, he reached out for her hand weakly, sad and urgent at the same time. "*The dear father would with his daughter speak, commands her service…*" he reached behind him and pulled out his top pillow, holding it out to her like a sacred offering. Claudia took it from him with trepidation, not exactly sure what he wanted her to do.

"*It is silliness to live when to live is torment, and then have we a prescription to die when death is our physician,*" he said gravely, pushing the pillow further into her arms.

Claudia jumped up from the chair, recoiling from the pillow like a snake. "No, no! I am not sure what you are asking, Dad, but I am not OK with this. Just hang on, I'll see about getting a nurse…"

She could see his frustration rising as he scrunched up his face for a final poetic salvo, searching through his mental Shakespeare index for the words to convince her, get his true meaning across to her.

"*Mine honour is my life; both grow in one; take honour from me and my life is done!*" he almost shouted at her, using up his last burst of energy and falling back against the bed, deflating in an instant. "*I love you more than words can wield the matter, Dearer than eyesight, space and liberty,*" he said so quietly that Claudia had to lean in right next to his face, picking up the pillow from the floor and attempting to set it back on the bed. He struggled against her for a moment, pulling the pillow down onto his face and placing her hand on top of it, his next words muffled and pleading.

"*Claudie, my love! Mercy!*" At the sound of her name, she lost all composure, her emotions a tangled jumble of edges and confusion. He hadn't called her by name since before his diagnosis, she often wondered if he even knew who she was anymore.

"I won't do it!" she yelled into the darkened room, "do you hear me, old man? You can't ask this of me, it's not fair!"

He looked up at her, tears falling down his gaunt face. He really was a dried out husk of his former self, she thought bitterly, recalling the robust, invincible man of her childhood. The cancer and the chemo had done their work all too well. He seemed hollow, fragile, like he was decaying from the inside out, having lost nearly fifty pounds since the illness began. She felt anger and guilt in equal measure, resenting her role in this Shakespearean tragedy, hating the choices he was forcing her to make.

"Where were you when I needed you, huh?" In her rational mind she knew she should stop, that she was unleashing years of pent up issues on a dying old man, but she didn't care. Not at that moment.

"All those years gone, wasted! And now when we are finally together, you pull me back in just to watch you die? Die and leave me. All over again. No, not just leave you want me to help you do it! What will that make me, Dad? How dare you!"

The clock on the wall above his head read just past two o'clock in the morning as she finished her last sentence, the words hanging angrily in the air like a toxic mist. She had never, in her entire life been more exhausted, more defeated. What on earth, she thought wildly, must he be going through?

"*Pray you now, forget and forgive,*" he said to her gently, his green eyes locked onto hers in a moment of complete clarity. She saw that the bond between them was frayed, fractured, but unmistakably present. Even after all that had passed between them, Claudia felt it like a physical pain.

"*The quality of mercy is not strain'd, It droppeth as the gentle rain from heaven. Upon the place beneath: it is twice bless'd; It blesseth him that gives and him that takes.*"

Claudia sat down heavily in the chair next to his bed, cradling her head in her hands. Her anger had drained away instantly, leaving only traces of adrenaline behind. She took several deep breaths, slowly calming her nerves before reaching out to take his hand. It felt like old parchment in her own hand, a baby bird's wing.

"Daddy, I…God, Dad. I am so sorry…" she stammered, searching for the right words. He was silent, unmoving, as she suddenly realized that she was talking to herself. The Bard was fast asleep.

Karen found her there the next morning, draped over her father's sleeping form. Claudia attempted to tell her what had happened, only leaving out the incident with the pillow. She decided to keep that private, exclusive of her and the Bard alone. Karen was curious, asking Claudia exactly what the Bard had said, as best she could remember. His words had jumped around so much between quotes and plays that the book became useless as a guide. Karen was saddened to hear of the poor man's suffering. They both knew that the Bard wanted his awful ordeal to be at an end.

After three days, Claudia imagined that what happened was all a dream, that he'd never awoken, never whispered he loved her or asked for her forgiveness. The Bard stubbornly held on, unresponsive, grasping at life as everyone around him marveled at his tenacity, but Claudia knew. Against all hopes she would be spared, she sensed he was waiting on a daughter's duty. A final act of mercy or complete insanity. Claudia couldn't decide which she would choose, preferred not to think of it at all.

"When this is all over, Kid, I hope we can go out and have a few drinks together," Karen said as she checked her sleeping father's ever-present vital signs, "maybe even more than a few, I'm thinking. The Bard deserves the tribute!"

Claudia stood and stretched to her full height, feeling older than she ever thought possible. She watched Karen lean down and gently kiss her father on the cheek, "God, I wish I would have known him before all of this, that I had seen him in his heyday," the nurse said sadly. "Oh, what might have been. Sleep well, sweet Bard."

"Thanks, K, you've been a godsend. I don't know if I would get through this without you," Claudia said simply. The women hugged fiercely, both of them grieving the Bard in their own way as Karen gave her a final squeeze and headed towards the door.

"I'll be back, Claudie. I'll finish my rounds then come sit with you," Karen said, "I don't believe it will be very long now."

Claudia sat back down, her mind in torment with her father's every labored breath. They were finally alone, father and daughter, once again. The Bard moaned, thrashing around weakly in his troubled sleep. Claudia crossed the room and went to her place next to the bed, took his hand and tried to calm him.

"I'm here Dad. It's OK, I will be all right. You can go now, you needn't be strong anymore."

One of the hospice nurses had been in earlier, upping his morphine, but Claudia knew. She could tell from the pained expressions on her sleeping father's face that it must be agonizing for him. How long would this last, this horrific limbo? She loved him, she realized in complete shock and wonderment. Against all odds, she actually loved him. She couldn't let him suffer anymore, would complete her final duty to him. Claudia reached over and gently removed the top pillow from underneath his head.

"You know, I never told you, but when I was a teenager, I came to your performance that time I called you. I sat in the last row," Claudia said to him, silent tears falling. Hugging the pillow tightly to her chest, she tried to muster up her courage. Claudia was to play Othello to her father's Desdemona, remembering a fatherless girl watching him perform onstage in a dark, half-filled theater. She was both fascinated and repelled by the murder in his eyes as he pretended to strangle his Desdemona, lost in his role, consumed by it.

"You were so powerful, so mesmerizing. A god of the stage, stealing every scene you were in; I didn't have the courage to meet with you like we'd planned. I just couldn't do it." she whispered into his ear, a final confessional as she stood and made herself ready.

"I was so proud of you. Proud I was your daughter, furious with you for the same reason. Angry that I needed you, that I loved you even though you abandoned me. How I love you still."

She lowered the pillow down to his face at the very moment her father's eyes snapped open, fixing her with his intense gaze. Startling green eyes, exactly like her own. He reached out to her, tried to speak, the words refusing to come. It didn't matter, Claudia understood all she needed to. The Bard took one last, deep breath, letting it out slowly as she laid the pillow down at his feet. Relief coursed through her as his soul took flight. He had given her the gift of life and now it seemed, he had also given her the gift of death. He had taken his final bow on his own terms, thank God. The consummate professional 'til the very end.

She placed his hand gently onto his chest and closed his sightless eyes, the last time she would ever look into them. His face was composed, finally at peace now that his final role had been acted out. Claudia felt years of anger and bitterness melting away, a butterfly emerging from its chrysalis at long last. She walked out of her father's room in search of Karen, testing out her new wings, eager and ready to take flight.

Originally published in "Storyteller Magazine" Volume 1/Issue 1 and reprinted in "Bewildering Stories," 2018

Blood Waltz

The skeletons were dancing. Their bleached appendages clacked and scraped together in a jumble of ulnas and tibias. They moved gracefully, in as much as skeletons could move at all, in perfect synchronicity. Harold Freeman stared at them in open-mouthed astonishment, a vague recollection of his schoolboy days dancing around the corners of his memory.

There are 206 bones in the human body. 270 at birth, that is, until the extra bones fuse together into the final number of 206. Harold, write this down, please!

Harold had never been much of an academic, but that random fact from Sister Mary Bernard's third-grade science class lingered in his mind as he watched the animated bones glide across the polished floor. This simply had to be some sort of dark dream, a wispy figment of his excellent dinner come back to torment him.

Harold was an elegant man of large appetites, the author of his own destiny who believed that moderation was for imbeciles. The way he saw it, you were either a victim or a predator and Harold had no desire to be someone else's lunch. He dined on the weak of mind, a first-class con man and thief. Dealing mainly with the old and infirm, the force of his larger-than-life personality always drew them into his various schemes and elaborate plans.

The last lovely lady had given him $52,000, the entirety of her life savings for his once-in-a-lifetime land deal before shuffling off this mortal coil. Although, she was helped along to paradise by a healthy regimen of poisoned herbal tea, served with tiny little finger sandwiches by none other than Harold himself. No one was ever the wiser—they never were. He'd lost count of how many had met a similar fate, preferring not to dwell on the unpleasant aspects of his chosen occupation.

He had a very refined palate, voraciously inhaling life's pleasures where and when he found them and needed a healthy income to keep them coming. Food was usually the first item on his list, followed by a taste for fine wines. At six-foot-five and tipping the scales at a hearty 377 pounds, Harold barreled through life eating up every second he possibly could. He wondered darkly if his own skeleton would dance on its own, buried as it was in layers upon layers of Harold, itching to shed him like a corpulent cocoon.

He was so engrossed with the skeletal couple, that he failed to take in the music that served as the backdrop for their ghoulish swaying. He chastised himself for the oversight. Harold was also quite the connoisseur of music, the classical pieces of yore tickling his fancy. He'd played the French horn in his school orchestra and could always pick out its plaintive, haunting sound in any performance. His ears perked up as he closed his eyes, feeling the crest and swell of the music. When he opened them again, he rubbed at his sockets furiously, not wanting to believe that what he was seeing was even remotely possible. An entire demented orchestra loomed before him, rotting, decaying corpses with instruments that appeared to be made of bone, muscle, and gore.

The conductor was something ripped from the pages of a Gothic novel, his left eye dangling down his desiccated face, wild brittle hair framing a countenance that would have been welcome at the very gates of hell. Over seven feet tall with his tuxedo moldering off of his half-rotted frame, the conductor held a large, razor-sharp femur bone in his right hand while keeping tempo with his left. He was very passionate about the music as pieces of him flew off in every direction, plopping softly onto the floor.

Harold knew that he had heard this music before, was trying to identify it as he also gazed in disbelief upon the orchestra. They ranged from skeletal to fresh, and every stage in between. The violinists were raw and angrily red, splashes of blood and carnage flying in their wake as they sawed away at their strings of sinew.

The flutists were delicate, mummified creatures, which Harold found endlessly amusing, for every flute player he had ever met in his band playing days was exactly that way in real life. Their brittle fingers worked upon the keys and he wondered how they could blow so well into their flutes, without a lip or nose to be found in the entire section.

He noticed that the trumpet players were a thing of macabre beauty. Black as pitch, they appeared horribly burned and disfigured. Hunks of charred flesh oozed off of their faces as they played, smoke billowing from red-hot instruments. Harold experienced a moment of ghoulish fancy, imagining the entire brass section engulfed in flames. There were many occasions when he'd wished fire and brimstone upon trumpeters, for they were a notoriously arrogant lot.

The rumbling of percussionists briefly caught his attention. A Lovecraftian vision, enormous slug-like apparitions with countless eyes were gripping their mallets in slimy tentacles, pounding away in fury. In between movements, they would reach out in their horrific grasp and snatch away pieces from the half-decayed woodwind players seated directly in front of them. Harold watched in disgust as one of the supernatural slugs gobbled down a mangled ear, slurping and smacking away in gruesome ecstasy without ever missing a beat.

The skeletons doubled back again, surprisingly nimble on fossilized feet as the waltz played on and on behind them. Harold had a moment of clarity, finally placing the name of the piece. *Of course! It was the "Wiener Blut," the Viennese Blood Waltz by Johann Strauss II. We played this many times in my orchestra, I should have recognized it immediately.*

In a display of pure fancy, Harold closed his eyes and began to move along with the hypnotic music. For such a portly man, he was incredibly light on his feet, twirling around the floor amongst the ghastly ensemble.

The waltz moved along to its stirring conclusion, a timpani drum roll with a full brass section that Harold was just itching to play again. He hadn't touched the French horn in years, but somehow he knew that he could do it, pick up right where he left off.

Faster and faster he spun, *one-two-three, one-two-three,* waltzing his imaginary partner around the floor as the skeletons struggled to keep pace with him. He was free, filled with glorious abandon as the music carried him along. As the very last notes washed over him, Harold paused and noted an empty chair in the brass section, exactly where he used to sit all those years ago. An enormous, blood-red French horn sat on the chair, glistening in bits of gore and huge, wriggling worms. One of the tiny creatures managed to extricate itself and began climbing up the leg of the player in the next chair. Harold took in the fact that his fellow horn player appeared to be half skeletonized already, the worms apparently doing their work all too well. Pieces of flesh still lingered *(upon him? Her? Harold really had no idea)* except for a full set of pulsating lungs that inflated and deflated like a balloon. It finished the final movement and gently placed the horn, bell down on its non-existent lap, turning to Harold expectantly.

He could hear the last notes of the piece still floating through the air, the hellish orchestra observing him, awaiting his reaction. The skeleton dancers stopped moving and stood completely still in anticipation. Always one to give credit where credit is due, even in the most distressing of situations, Harold began to applaud. At first tentatively and then with gusto. He cheered their efforts, for it truly was a masterful performance.

The conductor turned and took a final bow, his red eyes piercing Harold with malevolence. "Bravo! Bravo!" he said over and over as they basked in his admiration. The conductor stepped down off the dais and came face to face with him, close enough for Harold to detect an earthy, rotten smell with just a faint hint of sulfur. Harold could see, hidden in his unruly thatch of hair something he hadn't noticed before. Suddenly, everything clicked into place as he finally identified the knotted horns on the conductor's horrific head.

Harold had a sudden vision of a restaurant, an entire Chateaubriand all to himself with an impeccable bottle of a full bodied, 1985 Medoc Rouge. He raised a toast high into the air to celebrate the death of his latest mark, followed by a sudden, eye-watering chest pain. After that everything was a blur. *Or was it?* Harold quickly took stock of his life and knew that his prospects at the moment were greatly diminished, to say the very least.

He had only the briefest of moments to ponder his many sins before the conductor lashed out with his femur shiv and sliced cleanly through Harold's windpipe. Raising the bloody bone high into the air, Hell's orchestra rushed forward and slowly began to tear Harold apart.

It took them quite an age, for there was a lot of Harold to digest. They fell upon him in waves, feeding by each instrumental section until the entirety of the ballroom was covered in blood and discarded offal. The flutes and oboes each daintily gnawed upon a limb, pairing them down to the bone quite nicely in seconds as the bassoonists and trombones started in on Harold's ponderous stomach. The string section went in to liberate his well-worn liver while the slimy percussionists looped his large intestines around and around their hideous forms like shiny pink coats. The remainder of the string and brass sections fought over the scraps and Harold thought it only appropriate, since they were always jockeying for position within any ensemble.

Their grim task nearly at an end, the worms were unleashed to do their duty as they pruned Harold's considerable form down to the bone, leaving only his lungs untouched and in their proper place. He was grateful that he had never smoked a day in his life for his lungs appeared pink and full—ready to play for an eternity.

The orchestra moved back into position as the skeleton dancers considered this updated version of Harold, unencumbered as he was by gobs and gobs of superfluous flesh. They held out their hands to him as he rose from the floor, reborn into his true self at long last. He carefully made his way over to his new chair on bony feet, swaying wildly as he found his balance. He joined the dancers as they moved across the floor and back to their starting point.

Harold picked up his new French horn, the worms falling to the ground as he lifted it up to his freshly created skull and got into ready position. The conductor tapped his grisly baton onto his music stand, then raised it high into the air, signaling that they were ready to begin. Once again.

They would play the Blood Waltz. The creature that had once been Harold Freeman knew that it would always be the Blood Waltz. On and on in an eternal loop, as the orchestra played and the skeletons danced around them. As he took his rightful spot in the ensemble and began to play, Harold could feel the first pangs of gnawing, insatiable hunger as Hell's orchestra anxiously awaited its next inductee.

Harold might not dine well this night, but he knew that he would never dine alone again.

Originally published in "Ghostlight, the Magazine of Terror," Winter/Spring 2018 Edition and Dark Fire Fiction, June 2018

The Black Death of Happy Haven

The residents of the Happy Haven Retirement Community had no idea where the cat came from, just that he had been living there for as long as anyone could remember. His origins were a complete mystery. He was a friendly little fellow, jet black with four snow-white paws. He had a distinctive patch of white on his chest and nose making him look like he was wearing a tuxedo.

Old Mr. Dithers in 24C was the first to welcome him in, leaving bits of a half-eaten ham sandwich and a bowl of water outside of his door before heading off to breakfast in the cafeteria. For whatever reason, Dithers thought that the cat reminded him of his favorite bartender from his drinking days and decided to name him Frank. The name stuck, much to the endless amusement of the residents, that a cat named Frank lived among them.

The staff at Happy Haven attempted to shoo him out many times, but Frank always found his way back in, usually through a conveniently propped-open window. Of course, no one would ever admit to leaving one open. After a while, the nurses and office staff began sneaking treats and toys in their coats and bags, ensconcing the cat even further into the Happy Haven community. Frank became their unofficial mascot, prowling the halls in search of food and attention as the staff happily looked the other way. He loved the treats and home-made baked goods the residents shared with him, for he had a wide and voracious appetite.

Frank gave his affection freely among the residents, especially those who fed him. There were times though when Frank would latch onto one particular resident at a time, scratching at their door and meowing to get in. Once inside, Frank would stay by their side, insisting on sleeping on the bed right next to them. He would hiss if the nurse pushed him aside on her nightly rounds. The residents began to notice sometimes, the only way Frank would leave was when the person died.

Afterwards Frank would be on his merry way, back to his normal happy-go-lucky self until the next time. The residents would pop their heads out into the hall and see him there at a neighbor's door, howling to get in. It became the talk of the community, the more morbidly curious residents actually making bets as to whom Frank would attach himself to next. Everyone joined in, keeping a watchful eye, waiting for when Frank the friendly feline would morph into the "Black Death of Happy Haven."

Millie French was in a baking frenzy. She made the very best banana nut bread in the Haven, despite what old Marge and Rolly Gower said. Her secret? She used a whole stick of butter and special black walnuts instead of the regular kind. She and Marge had quite the rivalry going on, Marge constantly reminding Millie she was one of the lucky few in the building to still have a living husband. Millie had been a widow for over twenty years, Ed passing away from a sudden heart attack back in '96. She'd made her peace with it long ago, but the condescending way Marge would talk about her husband just set her teeth on edge (well at least her dentures, anyway.) Not that Rolly was any kind of prize. Millie was convinced he cheated at Yahtzee when he thought no one was looking. He would sometimes fall asleep during their weekly pinochle games, snoring loudly until his own wheezing would rouse him from his slumber, sometimes almost tumbling from his chair. Every single week.

Men were as rare as hen's teeth in the Haven. Millie and the other single gals were constantly bombarding them with dinners and baked goods in order to win their favor. The men in her building were taken care of very well, their bellies full every night as the ladies fussed and clucked around them like brightly-colored hens. Millie had her eye on a fella named George living one floor below hers, always sending him freshly-baked goods down on the elevator to let him know she was interested. That is, until the cat managed to eat half of the bread before George could even get to it, or the time before when some foul thief absconded with an entire loaf of banana bread and two dozen chocolate chip cookies. Millie couldn't be sure, but she was convinced it was Agnes in 44B. Agnes also had eyes for George and would never pass up an opportunity to spoil things for Millie.

Today Millie thought she would bring George the bread in person to make sure it arrived safely. She pinched her cheeks and added a dab of Chanel No. 5 behind each ear. She checked her reflection in the bathroom mirror, the overwhelming pink of the decor reflecting back at her from every corner of the room. Millie was very proud of her pink bathroom, had worked hard to find just the right pink matching towels, fuzzy toilet seat cover and matching accessories. It was the talk of the floor, everyone wanted to come in and see it, she thought happily as she fluffed up her curls and headed out for her impromptu date.

There was no way Agnes could possibly compete with this batch of banana bread. Millie had outdone herself. Maybe after she and George shared a slice or two, they could watch a little TV together. It was almost 4:30—the time for "Wheel of Fortune" to come on. The Wheel was must see viewing among all the citizens of Happy Haven—Pat Sajak was quite the celebrity around here.

Millie gathered up the bread and opened the door, excited and giddy as a schoolgirl. She turned to lock her door when a flash of black shot by her, just outside of her line of vision. Millie jumped, scrambling to get back into her apartment as Frank meowed and wrapped himself around her leg. Millie froze, waiting to see what the cat would do next. He merely flopped over and began to frantically wash his back left leg, lifting it high up into the air as only cats can do. She let out a long breath as Frank meowed, padding down the hallway, stopping for a quick bite of food two doors down. Her heart hammered in her chest so fast, Millie actually had to go back inside and sit down for a moment.

It's only Frank. He's not the Black Death, he's just a cat. Stop being so superstitious.

Millie retouched her face with an old compact she kept in her purse and took a deep breath, leaving a moment later.

There was no sign of Frank in the hallway as she cautiously approached the elevator doors while holding the banana bread in front of her like a talisman. She rode down one floor, letting the elevator music soothe her nerves. When the doors opened she turned to the right, mentally preparing for what she would say to George. Before she made it to his door, Millie suddenly stopped dead in her tracks. Frank was stretched out to his full length, frantically scratching and howling at the third door on the right. Hearing it sent shivers down her spine, the sound the cat was making was not of this world. He continued his terrifying serenade, doors opening up and down the hallway to see who the Black Death had singled out this time. Millie swallowed hard, her fear a lump in her throat. Tears began to cloud her vision as Frank continued to yowl and scratch away relentlessly at the Gowers' apartment door.

Millie felt horrible about Rolly and for every unkind thought about Marge as they sat in the cafeteria together after his funeral. Marge sat, deathly pale, as each resident of the Haven came to offer their sympathies. The kitchen staff would always decorate the cafeteria with pictures and tributes to the deceased. They laid out a spread of cold cuts, popcorn and cookies, served with overly-sweet lemonade in little plastic cups. It was a tradition at Happy Haven as their number continually dwindled, just an unavoidable fact of their everyday existence.

"It was a beautiful service," Millie said quietly to her friend, "I am so sorry, Marge. If there's anything I can do, please let me know."

"He would have loved it." Marge sniffled then blew hard into a large wad of used tissue. "It was so sudden, once he saw that cat, he was as good as dead!" She whispered fiercely into Millie's ear, looking around wildly in case Frank should suddenly appear.

Rolly had let him in, Marge told Millie in an angry hiss as the residents continued to pass by, giving her their condolences.

"That damn cat rubbed up against him and jumped onto his lap, there was nothing I could do!" Marge walked in the door and dropped her grocery bags, shocked to see Frank wrapped around her husband's neck. When Marge was able to pick him up and chase him back out into the hallway, the cat moaned and cried all night at the door until the neighbors began to bang on the walls in protest.

"It's OK, Margie. He likes me, see?" he told me, "There's no harm in it, just for tonight."

Marge watched as the cat curled up on her husband's chest, circling twice before settling in for the night.

"He would not budge, no matter what I did!" Marge exclaimed in exasperation. "I tried to stay up to keep watch, but you know me—I'm just no good after ten o'clock."

The next morning, she found Rolly sitting up in bed petting the cat, relieved beyond all measure that the "Black Death" was nothing more than a myth. When Marge finished her shower and stepped out of the bathroom, she found him.

Rolly was laid out on the floor, dead of a massive coronary. Marge wasn't fooled, she told Millie, not in the slightest bit. The Black Death stayed watch by his body, following the gurney out into the hallway as they wheeled him away before prancing down the hall in search of nourishment, a normal cat once again.

Martha Jane, affectionately known around the Haven as the "One-Eyed Knitter" for her prowess with the needles (even with only one functioning eye) came through the line, shaking Marge's hand and wrapping a long, baby-blue scarf around her shoulders. She was followed, much to Millie's annoyance, by George and Agnes offering joint condolences. Millie sighed heavily as they left the cafeteria together. She'd never made it to George's room, the cat shattering everyone's plans with his incessant caterwauling. *I might have to start from scratch, maybe this time with a homemade cheesecake, that ought to do the trick...*

"Millie!" Marge hissed at her through clenched teeth, "We need to talk!" Millie snapped her head up, she had been day-dreaming again, thoughts of George and baked goods running through her head. "We need to make plans, you have to help me!"

"Help you with what Marge? Something to do with Rolly?"

"Yes in a way. Something to help all of us in the Haven," Marge said, hysteria coloring her voice before lowering it to a deadly whisper. "You and I, we're going to get rid of that blasted cat once and for all."

Millie felt goosebumps break out all over at Marge's last words. A moment later the Black Death rounded the corner, locking eyes with them for just a moment before scampering off. They both sat in silent shock as a parting Frank let out a "meow" as if to acknowledge that the gauntlet had indeed, been thrown down between them.

Millie thought that her friend was really losing it. Marge obsessed about the cat morning, noon and night, plotting and scheming about how to get rid of him. Millie was loathe to tell her grieving friend most folks liked having Frank around. Some of the older residents appreciated having the heads up, many of them finalizing their end-of-life plans based on the cat's appearance at their door. He was a comfort to the sick, his soft fur and purring calming them. Whether or not he would single them out for his special attention didn't matter, they loved him anyway. He was feared by some but even so, Frank was simply part of the fabric of life at Happy Haven. Marge was convinced otherwise, her hatred all encompassing. Millie had never seen her friend so determined.

The first time Marge tried to catch Frank, she managed to lure him into a corner with a can of wet cat food. Once the hungry feline went for the bait, she sprung at him with a pillowcase, scooping him up in a great bear hug and flinging him out of the front door. He landed in the bushes, hissing and clawing through the cloth. Marge was convinced she'd finally saved the Haven from the Black Death. It was a short-lived victory.

The very next day they saw him making his usual rounds, stopping in front of Agnes' apartment for a quick bite. A week later, Marge convinced the UPS driver to take Frank out of the Haven and drop him at the local animal shelter, saying their building no longer allowed pets. Millie never knew how Frank managed to get away, but he was back three days later looking very satisfied with himself. He paused at Marge's door, letting out a loud meow on his way down the hall. It was on that day her friend became truly unhinged.

The rat poison was Marge's idea. Millie was against it from the beginning.

"Can't you see Millie? We will never be safe until that cursed animal is out of our lives! He is killing us in our beds!"

Millie was alarmed at how Marge looked, her eyes bulging and glazed over.

"Just make your banana bread and I'll do the rest—he goes crazy for banana bread! We'll leave it out in the hallway just for a little while, just a few bites and it will all be over. You told me you would help me, I need you now."

Millie eventually relented, Marge wearing her down. She reluctantly allowed her friend to sprinkle the white powder onto her famous recipe before placing it out into the corridor.

Marge called out to him, "Here, kitty, kitty!" as she headed down the hall to the elevator and the refuge of her own apartment.

Within minutes Millie changed her mind—she simply could not do it. She threw open the door and dashed into the hall, terrified she would find him eating the deadly bread. Millie felt faint, frantically looking in every direction. She couldn't believe what she was seeing. The banana bread was completely gone.

The neighbors around apartment 44B were beginning to get concerned. Agnes did not come down for Bingo on Tuesday even though she was supposed to call the numbers that week. Millie knew that Agnes would never miss the chance to be the caller, of that she was absolutely certain.

When Agnes didn't answer, they called in Haven management, the day shift superintendent using his master key to open the door. The One-Eyed Knitter told Millie they found her there on the floor, a trail of vomit and white powder streaking her face with a partially eaten loaf of banana bread on the floor next to her. Curled up on her back was the cat, both of them were lifeless as corpses but miraculously, still alive.

They never heard what happened to Marge after she was sent away, presumably to the nearest mental health center. They found her in her apartment raving about black cats and demons, a box of rat poison clutched in her hands like a weapon before the sedatives finally kicked in. Millie hoped that her friend had found peace and was finally receiving the help she so desperately needed.

Millie came clean about everything, her remorse was overwhelming. She visited Agnes every day in the sick ward, the two of them playing endless hands of gin rummy as Agnes recovered. Thankfully, she hadn't ingested much of the tainted treat. The cat had jumped out and startled her, causing her to drop the bread on the floor. Frank refused to leave as the sickness ravaged poor Agnes. They think the cat had eaten some as well, but not enough to kill him. The veterinarian's office had given him a clean bill of health.

Agnes and Millie decided, in the end, their friendship was worth more than any man. Besides, George had recently been seen in the game room eating homemade apple pie with Betty from 33D down the hall—the traitor!

The Black Death of Happy Haven was still seen around the hallways from time to time, but his roaming days were definitely over. Millie had permanently taken him in, feeding him three square meals a day, although she restricted his sweets (including her banana bread) to rare occasions. She made him his very own soft cushioned bed in the corner of her bedroom, but he only slept there during the day. Every night he would curl up in a ball and lay on her chest, the sound of his purring slowly lulling her to sleep. Once Millie had gotten through the first few nights, the curse of the Black Death stopped bothering her. She figured she was safe enough and besides, if it's your time to go, what better way than with a warm, loving friend snuggled up right next to you?

There are certainly worse ways to leave this earth, Millie thought as she carefully leaned over to avoid disturbing Frankie. She kissed him once on the head before turning off the light, settling in for a long and peaceful night in the Haven.

Originally published in "Adelaide Literary Magazine" and reprinted in "Pilcrow&Dagger," May/June 2018 edition

Lamentation

Even the sky grieved.

Gray and bleak, the wind cried out in lamentation, sending leftover pockets of old snow onto stark marble gravestones. Mourners passed by, eyes forward, each lost in their own world of respectful sadness. They walked along in silent groups, no one engaging in small talk or forced levity. Their task was much too grave for such normal pleasantries.

The enormity of what they were there to witness was etched onto every face. Time stood still as the horror of his mother's jagged screams followed the simple wooden coffin to its journey's natural end. The earth was piled high in anticipation, several shovels at the ready as they lifted and carried him from the conveyance. They lovingly placed rocks on the family headstone. One for every year of his short life and beyond, venturing into unmined decades never to come. A lifetime of promise gone in an instant as the wind kept up its relentless vigil.

Soft as a whispered prayer, his soul hovered in the wind. He couldn't comfort his father or still the tears of his poor mother, he could only observe from afar. A bystander to the final act of his brutally short life. He hadn't meant for things to go so far, never imagining a single rash decision would cost him so dearly.

The prayers were all said, the garments torn and rendered as one by one, they lined up to return him to the earth. Dust to dust, his brothers took up their sad burden. The first "shunk" of dirt landing on the coffin caused the assembled mourners to jump in alarm, the finality and irrevocable nature of the day overtaking them at last.

As they packed the earth down around him and said the final prayers, the sky opened up and grieved in earnest. The sleet came down in sheets, washing clean the obscene spectacle of a thirteen-year-old boy being laid to rest in the hard, cold ground of eternity.

The old man woke himself up with a start, he'd been having the dream again. It seemed to be getting more and more intense as he neared his ninety-third year. He never thought he would live this long, blessing the long ago day when the rope snapped and dropped him like a ton of bricks down onto the barn room floor. The troubles from eighty years ago had faded completely from his mind. He was damned if he could remember who or what had led him to such an action, only that he was extremely grateful at the outcome. Grateful for his long life.

Picture frames covered every inch of the room, his family bringing them from home for him to see. Children, grandchildren, two greats and one newborn great-great grandson adorned an entire wall. Next to them hung his high school graduation picture, his long deceased parents smiling with pride. He had been the first in his family to achieve such an honor.

An impossibly young man beamed out at his old eyes, uniform pressed and at the ready in the days following Pearl Harbor. A Congressional Medal of Honor adorned the space next to his military photo, given to him after he went back for several of his brothers on the blood-drenched shores of Iwo Jima.

A beautiful young woman in satin and lace looked up at his younger self in adoration, giving him over sixty years of love before taking her leave of this world. God, how he missed her!

The man continued to reminisce in the uneasy sleep of the very old, his large family surrounding him as he took his final breath. They all understood, even if he did not, how many were affected by his presence on earth. How many lives were created. How many were saved. How one life had made all the difference.

As he closed his eyes for the final time, the old man and tempestuous young boy were finally reconciled. Joined as one in eternal slumber, his soul took flight as the sky grieved and the wind cried out in lamentation.

Originally published in "Literally Stories," February 2018

An Appointment
With Mr. Dee

If you had to choose his very best characteristic (and there were so, so many), he would tell you that it had to be his ironic sense of humor. He was perhaps the most talked about, infamous representation of all of God's handiwork, enjoying his role in the grand scheme of things immensely. Sometimes, every now and then, all the good, important work he did threatened to bring him down. For although he was a celebrity in his own right, he did not always experience the adulation and credit that he felt was his due. At times, he was rebuffed, evaded, other times embraced and desired. It ran hot and cold, day in and day out always the same, the duality of his calling becoming more jarring to him with every passing year. If one could not find amusement in such a boring, maddening situation, really, what was the point of it all?

He considered taking a vacation, to try to "find himself" as they say. He knew that he was too invaluable to take any time off, (modesty admittedly not being one of his strong suits) so he decided to incorporate a part-time career into his busy existence.

For a while he played around with being a stand-up comedian, prowling the clubs on open mic night. The late hours got to be a little much, his famed droll sense of humor going over more than one head. Politics tickled his fancy for a bit, his peculiar talents being well suited for that bloodthirsty arena, but the sheer brutishness of it eventually repelled even him.

He was, at various times and in no particular order, a journalist, divorce attorney, aspiring YouTube star and card carrying member of the paparazzi, the latter profession utilizing his unrivaled ability to be seen and unseen, all at the same time. None of them lasted very long or ever filled the urgent longing residing in his heart.

If he were to be completely honest with himself (as he always prided himself to be), he would say that he was simply worn out. Maybe he was having a midlife crisis of some sort, searching in vain for any kind of self-fulfillment. He was never much for talking about his feelings, as much as he had any. In the end he decided to embrace the solution of the modern age. He went to therapy.

When Dr. Ethan Childs first saw the patient he came to know as Mr. Dee, he experienced a sudden feeling of deja vu, convinced that he had seen the man somewhere before. Mr. Dee assured him that they'd never met, that he simply evoked that reaction.

"My countenance is one that captivates or repels, occasionally at the exact same moment" the man said as he lowered his long, elegant form onto the nondescript black pleather couch in the corner.

Ethan prided himself on always putting his clients at ease, the gold standard of what a good psychotherapist should do. He was always professional, masking any random reaction to a particular client, making sure to never prejudge or make any assumptions. This time however, Ethan had to admit he was more than a little intrigued.

Dee always wore an expensively tailored suit, usually black pinstripe with a jaunty silken red pocket square expertly perched in his left breast pocket. He was tall—well over six feet, but carried himself with such a natural grace that his height was not intimidating. He had soft and well manicured hands, taking Ethan's own hand warmly into his in a firm handshake upon their first meeting.

Ethan couldn't place his age, guessed him to be in early middle-age due to his thick head of salt and pepper hair, but he could have easily been older or younger than that. The most striking thing about him was the polished black cane he always carried. It had an enormous gold knob at the top, a symbol that Ethan couldn't quite make out for he didn't want to seem rude and stare. With his confident air and refined stature, Mr. Dee would have fit quite nicely into any era. There was a certain timeless, classic quality about him.

Dee's voice had a slight lilt to it, an accent he couldn't quite place, piquing Child's curiosity even further. Ethan was discovering that he had to be wary, conversations with Dee were completely intoxicating. The man's razor-sharp wit and knowledge on a variety of subjects was extensive. They had long, impassioned discussions about history, philosophy and art, Ethan always attempting to steer Dee back to talking about himself, as the man would wax on poetically from one subject to another.

Mr. Dee had an uncanny way of turning every question or subject around so that Ethan would find himself fending off personal questions about his own life. This was something he knew was strictly forbidden, doubling his guard whenever Dee would steer the conversation in an uncomfortable direction. It was clear that Mr. Dee had experience in this kind of thing, telling Ethan, "I treasure confidences and pride myself on discretion. You can trust in me." More than once, Ethan had to remind himself that he was the therapist and not the other way around.

In the three months that Ethan had been working with Mr. Dee, he came to look forward to their sessions, found himself thinking about seeing the man with anticipation. Ethan tried to mentally step back and assess what was happening in his own mind. *Am I attracted to this man, is that what's going on?* The question tortured him late into the night.

Ethan's partner had died four years earlier from cancer, twenty years of life together passing by, seemingly in an instant. He felt the life drain away from his love as he sat by, day in and day out, powerless against death's relentless assault. Ethan was angry, still grieving. The pain lived like a dull ache just under the surface, coloring every aspect of his life. He'd refused to even consider dating again, much less ever develop feelings for a client. Ethan was extremely professional in every regard, would never dream of crossing that particular line.

He analyzed himself relentlessly, thought about seeing his own therapist about the dilemma before deciding that there was really only one solution. Ethan would have to stop treating the fascinating Mr. Dee, no matter how painful that would be for both of them.

Ethan spent the morning of their last session in a state of high anxiety. He really thought they had made some progress in the past few weeks, Mr. Dee was finally starting to open up. Dee refused to reference his childhood, even the slightest detail, except to say that he worked in a family business and had many diverse accomplishments to his name. He would never say exactly what that meant, but Childs knew that they were close to a major breakthrough, he could feel it.

Ethan rummaged through his desk, searching for his ever-present roll of Tums. His heartburn was particularly bad that day, the stress of what he had to do wreaking havoc with his body. He felt like he was coming down with something, physically sick about having to tell Mr. Dee that he would need to find another therapist. Ethan had put together a referral list for him, had it waiting on the desk as he practiced what he would say over and over again in his mind.

He had just gone over it once more when he felt a quiet presence move in directly behind him. It was eerie how Dee could enter a room in complete stealth, giving Ethan a physical shiver down his spine. He jumped up, completely caught off guard by the man's sudden appearance as Dee gently placed his hand on Ethan's shoulder, guiding him back down into his chair.

"There is no need to get up, Doctor, I already know what you are going to say." Ethan stared up at him, noticing that the symbol on the golden head of his cane appeared to be a large, grinning skull. "You see, I was afraid of just this very thing happening. I am an irresistibly charming fellow, another of my many positive attributes. Back in the Enlightenment years, I was a highly sought after guest. I think even old Ben Franklin had a thing for me then, ladies' man though he was, through and through."

Ethan felt a mild, warm sensation work its way from his toes all the way up to his chest and settle there. His mind was a blank, refusing to believe what Dee had just told him was real. Maybe this was all some kind of a strange dream.

"I am sad that our acquaintance must come to an end, Doctor. I have so enjoyed conversing with you. While I appreciate your graciousness in compiling a list for me, I have no further need of therapy. No other doctor will do and I am afraid that I just got the word from headquarters this morning, you are due to be processed momentarily." Dee pulled out an antique round timepiece on a golden chain, checking the time before clicking it shut and continuing on.

"Oh, the things you will see Ethan! I am a bit envious, I'm afraid. It is a blessing and a curse to always be wandering the earth. Life is beautiful and violent in all of its manifestations, I do tend to get rather attached to you all. I have become worldly throughout the long centuries—it is a particular fault of mine, you see."

Ethan felt the warmth in his chest suddenly explode, his heart seizing up as he desperately reached out, Dee placing a hand on each of Ethan's shoulders in a fond embrace. "My dear man, you are going on a wondrous journey. Do tell Jonathan hello for me."

In the midst of his pain and fear, Ethan jolted up at the mention of his partner, never having told Dee anything about him. He had a sudden realization of what kind of business Mr. Dee must be in, who he was; the breakthrough he had been after had finally occurred. It was his last conscious thought before the darkness began to close in around him, the sympathetic face of Mr. Dee bidding him farewell, his final sight.

Dee sighed and gently lowered his therapist's eyelids, arranging him in a dignified fashion. Ethan's next patient was due in about an hour, he would not be left unattended for long. Dee had really enjoyed their sessions together, it had amused him. He gripped his cane tightly, allowing his emotions to overcome him for just a moment, before leaving the office and closing the door softly behind him. Each passing both fed and diminished Dee, allowing him the sensation of approaching perfection without actually attaining it. All of life's infinite tragic comedy swirled around him, heartbreaking and euphoric as their souls ascended, passing him by, only ever allowing him to scratch at the surface of the grand plan like some sort of metaphysical lap dog. It was maddening, frustrating.

It was pure bliss.

Dee sighed in resignation. Such were the perils of his existence, had been since time immemorial. Maybe he should continue with therapy after all. He did appear to be in need of further exploration of his feelings—oh, how Dr. Childs would be pleased to hear that! A real breakthrough, if he did say so himself.

Dee stepped out into the bright sunshine, he had just over thirty minutes before his next appointment, a job interview with the local IRS office, was scheduled to begin. He was excited for this newest opportunity, knew it will be a perfect fit for him. *Oh, the irony!* he laughed to himself, whistling tunelessly as he sauntered down the street in pure contentment, therapy obviously agreeing with him. He was in good spirits, better than he'd felt in over a millennium.

For if there was one thing Death was certain he would be very, very good at—it was taxes.

Originally published in "Scrutiny Magazine," October 2017

I'll Get By

Viola lowered the lid with a strange sense of satisfaction as an angry creaking sound filled the air.

Even though she'd been doing this for as far back as she could remember, some nights were definitely worse than others. Dad really did a fine job on old Mrs. Johnson here— she looked like she was ready to get up and dance.

Dance! A sudden happy memory filled her mind of she and Loll kickin' up their heels at the dance hall last weekend. That new dance sure was the bee's knees! What was it called again? The Charleston?

A sharp chime from the antique Grandfather clock made her jump up in fright. Just ducky, nine o'clock already and she still had to finish the entire front parlor. Ma's not gonna be happy when she finds out I'm going out again tonight, she thought. Maybe she would sneak out once he got here, if she could catch him at the front door before he knocked, maybe her mother wouldn't hear?

Vi sighed dramatically. Ed. He has got to be the most handsome guy she'd ever seen, even dreamier than Francis X. Bushman. How she caught his eye instead of pretty little Loll, she never knew. He had the most beautiful hazel eyes and a thick head of jet black hair. Black Irish, he'd said he was, as he led her out to the floor.

Graceful and surefooted, they fit together like a glove, moving in perfect synchronicity without even having to touch. A snippet of her favorite song floated through her mind "I'll get by, as long as I have you..." as she began to sway in time to the imaginary music.

He's perfect in every way, she thought, now if he could only pass "the test."

Vi laughed as she remembered the first time she gave "the test" to an erstwhile beau. He'd followed her inside, eager to claim his good night kiss.

"Just a moment, Jimmy, can you help me with my nightly chore first?"

Man, he hightailed out of here like nobody's business, slamming the screen door behind him.

Vi wasn't just any old gal, she was a modern woman of the world, a true flapper. She and Loll were the founders the "Question Mark Cuties" complete with specially made question mark bathing suits in the new, risque style. Many a guy had tried to figure out just what that question mark meant, but none had ever been worthy.

She didn't have the time or patience for weak-kneed little boys; she was waiting for her very own Valentino to sweep her off her feet, steadfast and true. "The test" was a sure-fire way to weed out the bad ones, and she had given it countless times without any keepers.

Vi sighed again and headed over to the next coffin, gently pulling it shut over the peaceful face of the distinguished old gentleman inside. She heard a creak somewhere above her in their second floor residence. Is that Ma? She'd better hurry!

She sprinted over to the mirror in the front hallway, pinching her cheeks and fluffing up her short, bobbed hair. She remembered her mother's loud sobbing the day she came home with her daring new hairdo.

"Viola…your hair!" She could see the look of abject horror on the faces of her sisters and her brother's amused smile. Her mother angrily shooed her out of the house to go fetch her father at the local watering hole.

"Bring him home Vi, you just see what he does!"

She had never seen her in such a state, boy was she in trouble. She slowly walked the three blocks to where her father played poker with his friends. Her ma didn't like it, but Vi thought he needed a little down time, what with his job and all.

He was there in his usual spot, drinking something out of a cracked tea cup. I doubt that's tea, she thought, smiling fondly at him. He looked up, a momentary shocked expression clouding his face before he smiled at her, resigned to the situation. She was his favorite after all, he could never be cross with her for long.

"I see you went ahead with it Vi, I can only imagine your poor mother. Come on, sit with us awhile, I am in no hurry to get back now."

Vi was snapped out of her memory by a quick rap on the door, he's here!

She dashed down the hall as quietly as possible and pulled the door open without a sound. She was greeted by a single red rose held by a very dashing young man. Vi swallowed hard, moved aside to let him enter.

"Hiya kid, you ready to paint the town?"

She accepted the rose, looking up into those mesmerizing eyes. She had never seen eyes quite that color before and she swore she could see her future in them. Vi made an instant decision and took his hand to lead him out into the cool night air.

"Sure thing Ed, let's hit the road."

Before she could close the door behind them, he stuck his foot out and headed back inside.

"Aren't you forgetting something?"

She watched in open-mouthed astonishment as he walked into the main parlor and began to close each coffin, one by one. He did it respectfully, looking at each occupant with reverence before shutting them in for the night. His task completed, he turned back and gave her a long, passionate kiss. She felt weak in the knees, her own Sheikh of Araby here at last.

He broke away and winked at her, "So did I pass?"

For the first time in her life, Vi was rendered completely speechless.

"Now, about that question mark…"

Vi couldn't be sure, but she was convinced she could hear the strains of "I'll Get By" gently floating on the breeze as they walked arm and arm out into the night and into her future.

Originally published in "Flash Fiction Magazine," March 2017

Suspicious Minds

The clouds were moving. If Harvey closed one eye, he could see them as they drifted above him. He didn't know when dental offices began putting relaxing pictures in their light fixtures, but he was damned grateful for it. It could have been the numbing stuff they jammed into his gums or that he had been in this chair for an hour and was starting to hallucinate, but those clouds were definitely moving.

He tried closing the other eye and focused on a palm leaf in the far corner of the frame. It was supposed to simulate lying on a beach, looking up into a summer sky. Anything to calm the suckers. This dental office was a bargain basement deal, run down but good enough for his purposes.

Harvey Walter sucked in a deep breath and tried to calm his nerves. The well-endowed dental assistant made him bite down on some nasty, sticky stuff to get an impression for a crown. He'd been sitting here for over five minutes with his mouth clamped shut in the goo. She had just filed his bad tooth down with a high-pitched saw, the vibration still echoed through his brain.

The worst part had been the smoke. It wafted up out of his mouth like a brush fire as flakes of tooth fell down his throat, causing him to gag. Now as he waited for the skirt to come back, he cursed the miserable bastard he called a sperm donor for saddling him with these awful gums and teeth. He never knew much about his father other than he had bad dental hygiene. The man had a full set of dentures by the time he was thirty, or so Harvey heard.

What a legacy it was. Two crowns, four cavities and a root canal for his troubles just this year. He was certain next year there would be a new set of hellish problems, regardless of how many times he brushed and flossed. Then they would charge him a small fortune to poke around his mouth with their high-powered torture devices.

Harvey Walter was cursed, there was no way around it.

The perky assistant came back in and extricated his diseased choppers from the tooth cement. It made a sickly, sucking sound as she worked it out, back and forth, again and again until it came free. Her breath smelled like oranges and Harvey wondered again what he could do to get a more private session with her.

He highly doubted she would go willingly. He was on the north side of fifty with bad teeth and an evolving financial situation. "No" had never stopped Harvey before, maybe he could hang around the parking lot for a while when he was through. His loins tingled in anticipation as she squirted a healthy dose of water into his mouth and told him to spit. She said the main guy would be coming in to see him in a minute. In the meantime, he should try to relax. Like that was even possible.

Harvey concentrated on the cloud again, watching as it changed from the shape of a dog into an angry woman. He thought he was losing his mind as he watched the cloud woman's face open into a blood-curdling rictus of a scream. He could see her eyes bulging out in terror, a moment of exquisite human pain before the cloud changed back again. Harvey was almost sad to see her go. Pain was a specialty for him, he was a real artist.

The picture was electronic or something. A way to distract him from the fact that he was stuck in this horrible place. He watched as a small burst of wind caused the cloud to drift from the picture then closed his eyes and imagined being on that beach.

Man, wouldn't that be something? Maybe after he fenced the stuff from his latest job, he could take a vacation, go somewhere tropical. After he spent a little quality time with the dental assistant, that is. He thought he still had some rope in the trunk if she couldn't be persuaded by his charms. He almost hoped she would fight, it was always more exciting that way.

Harvey was floating on an errant cloud. He felt dizzy, positively giddy as the wind blew through what was left of his hair. Music, loud and rumbling came at him from somewhere far away. A bass guitar, the driving beat of drums. Saxophones? It was a rock anthem, he could almost place it. It was getting louder, coming at him from all directions. The cloud dissipated mid-air, sending him plunging to earth at a breakneck speed.

Harvey jolted himself awake. He was still hanging backward in the dental chair, almost completely upside-down. A line of drool escaped his gaping mouth and hit the floor. He had a brief recognition that a lot of time had passed since the skirt had left him, he could see the dusk of late afternoon seeping through the lone dirty window in the corner. Loud rock music was piping in through the ancient speakers in the ceiling. Classic 70's rock, the kind of drivel his old man would jam out to in between benders, back in the days when he was still around.

"We're caught in a trap, I can't walk out.....because I love you too much, bab-ee!"

Harvey could almost picture his father, a bottle of Rheingold clutched in one sweaty hand. A transistor radio blaring out in the garage where the old man did his serious drinking, beer bottles lined up end-to-end on his beat-up workbench like a row of dominoes. Harvey always wanted to knock them over, just to see how they would fall. Not that he would ever dream of doing such a thing. When it came to beatings, his old man was a bona fide expert. It was another thing they apparently had in common. Besides rotten teeth.

Blood was rushing to his head and he had to take a serious piss. He'd been so distracted by the memory of his father that he failed to notice his chest and arms were painfully tied to the chair. He recognized the rope from his car, fashioned into good solid knots that held him down, completely immobile. He wrenched his head to the side trying to get his bearings. A single blue sequined shoe came into his line of vision, first one then another.

"Why can't you see what you're doing to me...when you don't believe a word I'm sayin'..."

Harvey followed the shoes up, his neck screaming in agony as he took in what surely was a nightmare. The man towered over him, enormous in every way. A blood-stained, white jumpsuit held his rolls of fat together like a giant sausage casing. Four or five chins bent over Harvey, oversized purple sunglasses rimmed in gemstones covering the man's face. Harvey was thankful for them as a fat, wriggling worm worked its way free from the man's left eye frame, landing on Harvey's chest with a sickening plop. The telltale smell of meat left out too long in the sun assaulted his nose as the man took a huge, squalid breath and blew hot, rancid air into Harvey's face.

"Hey there, son! What's shakin' bacon?"

The dental assistant suddenly loomed over him, or at least Harvey thought it was her. Her face looked like someone took a bag of hammers to it. Her right eye dangled halfway down her cheek taunting Harvey as she giggled like a schoolgirl. She cleared her desiccated throat to speak, loudly and otherworldly, into the darkened room.

"Ladies and Gentleman! Prepare yourselves for The One, The Only! The tartar trouncin', cavity exterminatin', King of the Crowns....one bad-ass, sick mamma jamma.....it's....The Dentist!"

A sickly yellow spotlight lit up the Dentist as he rose to his full height. The assistant squealed with delight, clapping and swooning in ecstasy. A chorus of "Glory, Glory Hallelujah" rang out into the room, the Dentist holding his arms out to recognize his adoring fans. Harvey didn't know if they expected him to clap. Not that it was possible since they had him trussed up tighter than a Thanksgiving turkey.

"Thank you! Thank you verra much!"

Harvey opened his mouth to speak, emitting nothing but a hoarse squawk for the effort. The Dentist turned his attention away from the spotlight and gave Harvey a gruesome smile. A single golden tooth in a mouth full of blackened rot beamed out at him and Harvey had the crazy thought that maybe the man should brush and floss more.

"No, son, don't get up. C'mon darlin', let's fire it up!"

The dental assistant's voice spoke low and softly into his ear, a voice filtered through a mouthful of dirt.

"Still want to get together, hon?"

The high-pitched drill went off again and this time, Harvey had a sinking feeling that smoke would be the very least of his worries. She held it high over his head, cackling with savage laughter before lowering it to his face. Harvey clamped his mouth shut as the Dentist dove in and pried his jaw back open. The Dentist's enormous diamond ring lodged directly in Harvey's eye socket, the smell, and feel of the man's greasy hands causing him to gag. The assistant jammed the drill into his exposed tooth nerve as the music blared on above him.

"*We can't go on together, with suspicious minds! And we can't build our dreams on suspicious minds!*"

Every part of Harvey jolted in electric, excruciating pain. He flopped around like a hooked fish, the rope holding him fast to the chair as she continued to dig in with the drill. He could feel the blood filling his mouth as she moved on to the rest of his teeth.

The last thing he saw before passing out was the light fixture. It was flowing crimson with blood. The clouds formed into broken, demon-like creatures, their open mouths extended into silent screams. Harvey recognized it for what it surely was—the very portal into hell.

Harvey came to slowly, the bright chair light hovering directly over him. The Dentist was poking around in his tortured mouth with a sharp instrument. The assistant stood off to the side, stringing Harvey's battered teeth onto a long necklace. A trophy for the King of the Crowns. Harvey certainly wouldn't be using them anymore. He could feel the throbbing stumps with his tongue, the jagged shards of brutalized teeth sticking up here and there as the Dentist fussed and scraped away at them.

At last, the Dentist appeared satisfied and the music mercifully stopped. He ran his hands through his oily, pompadoured hair and let out a dispirited sigh. Harvey was glad for brief reprieve. Maybe now that the teeth were gone, his ordeal would finally be at an end.

"I'm sorry, son. The rot goes even deeper than we first thought. I'm afraid we are going to have to get it all out."

The assistant lovingly draped Harvey's teeth over the Dentist's bloated neck. He reached out to gently touch her cheek, the skin sloughing off into his hand. Harvey had only a moment to wonder what rot could be left in the barren wasteland that was his mouth before the Dentist turned his attention back to the job at hand. The music started up again at full volume, sending Harvey into a fit of sudden, bright laughter.

"So if an old friend I know, drops by to say hello, would I still see suspicion in your eyes.."

In answer to his unspoken question, the Dentist turned around and fired up a blood-spattered old chainsaw, holding it up for his inspection. The spotlight came on again framing the man in all of his deranged glory. Harvey, screaming with laughter, lifted his head as far as it would go in one last act of defiance. The dental assistant swooned anew, oohing and aahing at the Dentist's every move. A consummate professional, one bad-ass, sick mamma-jamma was the Dentist. Harvey found he actually admired him a little.

The Dentist lowered his chainsaw and went back to work.

Victoria Cole made sure to swab down the dingy old chair with a sanitizing wipe before deigning to sit in it. She hadn't planned on coming here. An old crown had broken suddenly, forcing her to settle for this awful place in an emergency. It had happened at dinner, right after the last course, as she gleefully watched her ancient husband convulsing on the floor.

She had done her research, making sure the poison she used was undetectable. So far, no one seemed any wiser. Her husband was of an advanced age with pretty severe heart problems so there really was no need for suspicion. Victoria was about to come into a very large inheritance. She had serious plans to make, but only after she got this stupid tooth fixed.

"We're caught in a trap, I can't walk out. Because I love you too much, ba-bee!"

Perfect. Her tooth situation was upsetting enough without annoying old rock songs ringing in her ears. God, how she hated dentists. They really were a necessary evil.

The cheap looking dental assistant came in smacking a wad of sweet-smelling pink gum. She said the dentist would be right in, he was just finishing up with another patient. Victoria leaned all the way back in the chair and studied the strange beach picture frame stuck over the ceiling light. She wasn't sure, but it looked like things in the picture were moving.

She closed her eyes in a light doze and smiled, the warm feeling of fresh widowhood spreading over her. They would put the crown on and then her new life would begin, she just had to get through it. She had somehow survived five years of married life with the old man, she could certainly do this.

After a while, she heard heavy footsteps behind her, her eyes instantly snapping open. She noticed the picture had changed. There was a large cloud forming, the face of a portly, shrieking man. A sudden streak of red slashed through the blue sky, bloody and ominous. The abrupt voice of the dental assistant directly behind her made her jump. Fully awake now, Victoria tried to get up and realized that she was tied down to the chair. Like a rat caught in a trap, she began to pull at the restraints in a sheer, animalistic panic.

"Ladies and gentleman, the Dentist has entered the building!"

Like nails on a chalkboard, the drill went off somewhere in the room, its high frequency piercing her sanity. Screaming hysterically, a seedy golden spotlight lit up the room and Victoria somehow knew she was about to face her judgment.

The blood-soaked faces in the light all smiled in anticipation, waiting for their newest member to join them. The thing that had once been Harvey Walter was among them, hungry and feral, as was his nature. A true showman, the Dentist preened and posed in the spotlight, basking in their joint terror and endless adulation.

"We can't go on together, with suspicious minds!"

The King of Crowns swayed briefly to the music then picked up his instruments and went back to work.

Originally published in "Literally Stories", December 2017

The Cat

The cat extends himself to his full length, peeking through the window. He lets out a hearty meow, shattering the tomb-like silence of the old house.

He is a funny looking little creature, a black koala bear nose nestled on a white face, like negative film exposed too long in the light. He has a patch of black on one leg, another completely white. His black and white, yin and yang markings swirl around in confused, disorganized perfection. The very epitome of what a molly gowser, short-haired, respectable alley cat should be.

He prowls the perimeter of the house, drawn to it by some inexplicable instinct that makes him yowl in feline delight. Having no luck at the front window, he heads around to the back door, scratching and clawing at it in his impatience.

Anne jumps up with a start, almost dropping the crystal wine glass she had been cleaning. *What is that unearthly sound?* She sets the glass back down on the dining room table and sighs at the sight. Glasses, dishes, pots and pans, cups as far as her eye can see sit out on every surface, waiting to be organized.

In fact, the living room is completely filled, every inch covered with clothing, Tupperware, cooking utensils, loose bits of bric-a-brac—the contents of an entire life, unvarnished and on full display.

She sighs and picks up the fortifying glass of wine on the counter, taking a big sip. *There is no way that I can ever get through all of this, she thinks in despair. I don't even want to.* The Estate Sale is tomorrow, the day of reckoning. She has put out the signs, the ads have been posted and reposted, now all she has to do is throw the doors open and sell all of her childhood memories to complete strangers. *What's not to love about that?*

The cat gets no response at the back door but he is not deterred.

He rounds the garage and sees a large picture window, light streaming through. He gets a running start and launches himself onto it with claws fully extended. He hits it at full speed, a loud crunch breaking through the thick window pane, before landing hard in the bushes.

He slinks away to regroup, truly embarrassed in the way that only cats can be, at anything less than complete gracefulness.

Anne is amazed at the folks she has met coming and going in her parents' house today. She would never have expected to find so much goodness, followed by sheer greed. More than one person wanted to give her a hug and share their stories, while another special soul offered to buy her father's military coffin flag for $10.

They rifled through every part of this place, looking for items even in the medicine cabinets, hall closets, drawers, kitchen cabinets, spices—nothing was off limits. It was a huge success, as far as these things go, so why do I feel like I need a shower?

Anne drags the last few bags down to the end of the driveway.

This is it she thinks, the last of it, going off to Goodwill. It is finally over. A flash of something white catches her eye and speeds off into the bushes. *What was that, a rabbit?* The bush emits a loud meow, as if in answer to her unspoken question.

Anne immediately feels a pang of guilt. Her mother had three cats, and she had to find a home for them. *There was no way I could take them all and the older two were a package deal, having been together their entire lives.* A nice young couple had come over in response to her animal rescue posting and taken the pair of old Maine Coon Cats off to their new, and hopefully happy, home.

God, getting them packed up and into the car was heartbreaking, they had lived in that house for over 10 years. Those cats were everything to Mom, filling her life in the years after Dad died.

Anne makes a quick decision and heads back into the house, searching for her mother's supply of dried cat food.

The cat, having just finished his second midmorning nap, takes one last, luxurious stretch and ventures out of the bush in search of food. He can smell something in the air, he is an expert in these things, and follows it eagerly around to the front porch of the house. Seeing the source of his good fortune, he rushes forward and falls upon his prey, crunching and gulping in pure feline ecstasy.

Anne tries to stifle a giggle as she watches the cat gorging on the small bowl of food. She furtively peeks through the screen door, not wanting to scare him away.

He has to be the strangest looking cat she has ever seen, with his unique markings and her heart goes out to him in his hungry state. She notices that his tail curls, all black except for the white patch on the bottom, and that nose!

She doesn't know why she thinks he's a boy, she just seems to know it. In all these years she has never seen him before. He must have wandered into the neighborhood from the local dumpster, he is so filthy. Even in his disheveled state, she can see that he is still pretty young. Probably the by-product of an unwanted kitty union, one of the many forgotten creatures of this world.

An orphan, she thinks, just like me.

Anne feels a chill run through her at that last thought, as the cat looks up and locks eyes with her. He immediately springs into action, meowing and scratching at the screen door, trying to get to her. *What harm could it do? She asks herself, this has always been a haven for cats after all.*

The new carpeting has just been installed, but if she keeps him on the front tiled entryway, she could let him in for just a minute. She tentatively pushes the screen door open and jumps back as the cat shoots forward like a rocket, leaping into her Mom's favorite chair, circling twice before curling into a ball and laying down.

Tears spring to Anne's eyes—she can almost see her mother sitting there, a cat in her lap and a glass of wine in her hand while watching Monday night football. The cat purrs loudly and looks up at her, his amber eyes shining. She reaches out and strokes his head as he kneads in delight, making himself completely at home, as only cats can do.

If this isn't a sign, I don't know what is, she thinks as she catches a sudden whiff of her mother's favorite perfume. For the first time in what feels like an eternity, she is completely at peace.

"You're quite the independent little guy" she says to him, "I think I'll call you Indy."

The cat can't put it into words, he is a cat after all, but he instinctively knows that he belongs with them. He knows a cat person when he sees one and the silver haired lady with the kind face is definitely of his tribe.

Every night he has heard her calling out to him "Here kitty, kitty!" from across a great distance and has been following her voice for days now, across many miles. He can see her inside, sitting in a chair behind the younger woman that he already knows as his new person.

Jumping up onto her lap and receiving affection from both spiritual and earthly beings, as is his due, the cat is finally content. His new person will do fine just as long as she remembers to keep feeding him dinner.

Anne takes a final look at her childhood home, all freshly painted and cleaned out. This moment is bittersweet, but she knows it will be OK.

She turns and locks the door, the real estate agent will begin the first showings in the morning and they are confident it will sell right away. She bends down and picks up a freshly bathed Indy, tucking him under her arm as he purrs happily. Her husband is going to kill her, but Indy will win him over, she loves him already.

This is going to be the beginning of a beautiful friendship, kid, just like the old movie says.

She gives him a quick kiss on the head before getting into the car and taking him to his new forever home.

The silver haired lady watches them as they drive away, satisfied that her final task has been completed. She backs away from the front window as the curtain gently settles back into place, as if moved by an invisible breeze.

Those two are a match made in heaven, she thinks, and *I know my daughter will be OK.* With heaven on her mind, she takes her leave of this world, excited and ready for her new adventure to finally begin.

Originally published in "Peacock Journal," October 2016 and "Write to Meow Anthology," May 2018

Momma Said

Helen Wilson was at the end of her patience. The absolute end. For three days running the little boy would run up and down the hallway, laughing and playing right at the break of day, scaring Helen out of an uneasy sleep. She had traveled a long way to escape her troubles and indulging the whims of a child was simply not in her plans, only served to remind her of all she had lost. She craved peace and quiet, in that order. So far, her stay had been anything but peaceful and there was definitely nothing quiet about the boy.

As his noisy footsteps tapered off away from her room and down the hall, she laid back and tried to make sense of her new reality. A reality in which she no longer had a husband. She remembered, so clearly, that last phone call from Michael. She had just recovered from her latest miscarriage. Physically they told her she was good to go, but she was completely devastated in every other way, the simple act of getting out of bed each morning becoming a monumental challenge. It was the third baby they had tried so hard for and lost in a dramatic, red flourish. The final one putting her into a hospital bed at 3 o'clock in the morning. She'd driven herself to the ER since Michael was out of town on a business trip, was always out of town on a business trip.

"Helen, I love you. I will always love you, but I just can't go through it all again," Michael said, anguish coloring his voice. *"I just can't. I'm so sorry honey."*

They had gotten married later in life, both of them professionals with busy lives and full schedules. They were always putting off having kids, chocking it up to career obligations until Helen could literally hear her biological clock ticking like a bass drum. It was so loud and relentless that it kept her up at night, contemplating her own mortality. She told herself that there was still plenty of time; "older" women were having healthy babies all the time, there was no need for concern.

The first time she suspected that she might be pregnant she and Michael were in Maui on a rare vacation, cell phones turned off and put away. She had gone down to the local ABC store and purchased a pregnancy test. Nervously she sat in the bathroom of their hotel room waiting for the results, rocking back and forth on the covered toilet seat in some sort of anxious ritual. When the line turned blue, she stared at it in awe, silent tears running down her face before running back out to the convenience store. She bought three more tests, each showing the same positive result, a vindication of their quest for a baby. She chilled a bottle of champagne and told him while they sat out on their balcony, overlooking the ocean at sunset. Michael was crying tears of joy as he swept her up into his arms and danced her around the room. It was the most perfect moment of her life.

One month later it was all over. Helen convinced herself that she was working too hard and that next time, she would do things better. Michael put on a brave face, throwing himself into his work even more, traveling five days out of seven for out of town sales trips. On his weekends home, they would try again, Helen studying up on fertility charts, constantly monitoring her daily temperature in the hopes that the limited time they had together would be successful. Romance became a chore between them as Helen pursued her goal with the single-minded determination that was the hallmark of her life—if you're going to do something, you go all in or not at all.

Finally, after another six months passed, Helen announced that she was expecting again. This time it was a much quieter affair, both of them cautiously optimistic. Michael was afraid to show too much emotion, fear and happiness waging a war across his face as she sat quietly and told him of their good fortune.

She had so many plans, was arranging to spend her last trimester on leave from her law office. She was meticulous in her habits, watching every movement and bite of food, but in the end it made no difference. She miscarried the following week.

Helen was jolted out of a light doze by a loud tapping on her hotel room door. The clock on the nightstand read just past five o'clock in the morning as Helen blearily rubbed her eyes, trying to clear the corners of her vision. *Where on earth are his parents, allowing him to carry on this early in the morning?* A second loud thwack hit her door as she angrily got out of bed, having just enough time to fasten her robe before throwing the door open in a sudden rush. She expected to see him standing there, her mind already forming a picture of what he must look like, but the hallway was completely empty. She turned to go back into her room when a flash of bright color caught her eye and she found, sitting right outside of her door, an enormous blue Cat's Eye marble.

With the marble in her robe pocket, Helen shut the door and leaned up against it for a moment. She could feel a migraine beginning to form behind her eyes, knowing that she would need to take a couple of ibuprofen quickly or the entire day would be unbearable. She found the pills on the nightstand and quickly washed them down with the remnants of last night's scotch glass, Michael's favorite brand that they used to drink together in happier times. She crawled into bed and tried desperately to fall back asleep.

The third time, she knew she was pregnant before she even took the tests, confirming it with a hastily arranged trip to the OBGYN. The doctor had sent her to a specialist after the second miscarriage, running every test known to man: DNA, blood tests, lab work, a complete barrage of miraculous modern medicine. After all of that, they could still find nothing wrong with her, other than the fact that she had just celebrated her forty-second birthday, the infamous clock pounding away, slowly breaking her heart. Michael was also reluctantly tested, looking like a man walking off to the executioner as he entered the clinic, somber and pale. His results were completely normal as well, there was no earthly reason why they couldn't reproduce and carry a baby to term. Helen doubled down, began taking fertility medicine and vowed to try even harder.

Another year passed, another birthday. They began to fight over little things, daily annoyances turning into big blow-ups as Michael retreated ever farther away from her and into his work. Neither one of them was happy, but they carried on in an uneasy truce until the day the doctor told her the miraculous news that she was indeed, pregnant once again.

This time, there were no tears of joy, champagne or even her husband. She told him over the phone while he was at the airport getting ready to board the red-eye flight to LA. He was thrilled, he told her, would be home as soon as he could, but she could tell his heart just wasn't in it anymore. After so much disappointment, she knew that he was afraid to be hopeful. Sometimes, in the darkest hours of the night when she was being completely honest with herself, she had to admit that she felt exactly the same way.

As the first month turned into the second, Helen began to believe that they may have turned a corner. She began to cautiously make plans for the future, looking online every morning to see what stages of development her baby was in from week to week. One week, it was a tiny cluster of cells, another and it was beginning to develop into a vaguely human-like shape. She endlessly researched websites and medical journals, tracking her progress as the weeks went on. They finally planned to tell their friends and family after the twelfth week had passed.

Helen began to speak to the baby, her "beloved parasite" as she liked to call him. She wasn't sure how she knew he was a boy, she was just convinced it was so. She started to take time off from work, assigning her cases to the junior partners, slowly extricating herself from her daily routine. Michael spent more time at home as well, smiling and laughing with her again as she began to feel the first flutter-like motions of her baby boy, like a butterfly trapped in a glass.

By the end of her first trimester, they began to paint his room. Helen insisted on a robin's egg blue, convinced that their son would have blue eyes the exact same shade of the morning sky... Michael's eyes. She was feeling wonderfully maternal, picking out a crib and just the right curtains to match the baby's bedding. Her mother in Colorado was unable to visit due to ongoing health issues, but sent Helen an entire set of sheets, blankets and decorations all in a Noah's Ark theme. Pairs of animals graced his blue walls, smiling happy creatures that would welcome him into this world with all the joy and love she already felt for him displayed in every corner. Her precious baby, her boy.

Every night, especially when Michael was away, she would sit in the baby's room with the lights on low, listening to the tinny music of the wind-up mobile, the soft, plush lions and bears spinning slowly above his crib, every item lovingly placed and waiting. She had read that after the first trimester, the chances of carrying to full term were greater and she silently celebrated as she passed that milestone, calling Michael eagerly to share the news. They talked about names for the first time, Michael insisting that they include some options for girls even though Helen knew that wouldn't be necessary. She had a feeling about his name, knew that he would tell her in his own good time what his name was...

"*Willie!*" a voice whispered into the darkened room causing Helen to jolt straight up in the bed, clutching the blankets around her like a frightened child. "Hello? Who's here?" she said out loud in a firm voice, trying to tamp down the shock and fear pulsing throughout her body.

"Come out now!" She reached out and flipped on the lamp in a panic, the harsh light filling the corners of the room to reveal that she was all alone. Completely and utterly alone.

Helen sighed and decided that last shot of scotch was a mistake, she was obviously hearing things. She reluctantly got up and put on a pot of coffee, deciding a hot bath was just what she needed to begin her day. As the hot water flowed over her, she broke out into great gulping sobs, holding herself and rocking back and forth as the steam rose up and enveloped the antique claw-foot bathtub. Helen was so lost in her grief that she never even noticed the bathroom door as it swayed back and forth several times before softly closing, all on its own.

To say that she mourned his loss would be a complete understatement. By the time Helen reached the hospital on that horrible night, she began to despair for she was in the third week of her second trimester and the pain and carnage were frightening. She vaguely remembered them telling her at some point that the baby was gone, all was lost, before sedating her into blissful darkness.

Michael rushed home as soon as he heard, but it was all over by the time he got there. He found her, face turned towards the wall, refusing to even meet his gaze. Helen was somewhere else entirely, in a world where their baby still existed. He couldn't reach her, he tried for awhile, but the writing was on the wall and they both knew it.

Helen took a leave of absence from work after that; arguing cases no longer held much appeal for her in her grief and she began to wonder why she ever thought any of it was so important in the first place. Michael cleared his schedule to take care of her, Helen walking through her days in a black haze. Michael tried his best, Helen knew that and loved him for it. He had begged her forgiveness for not being there in her time of need and held her late into the night when the tears would spring up out of nowhere. He talked about adoption, but Helen was not ready to think about it, couldn't even hear it.

After a few months had passed, she began to believe that her son would come back to her, that his little soul was out there waiting in some kind of heavenly holding pattern. They just needed to try one last time and he would come, she was certain of it. She told Michael that she was ready to try for a baby again as he sat silently beside her holding her hand, the color draining from his face. The very next day, he packed his bag and left for a sales meeting across the country.

The day after that, he called and told her he wanted a separation.

The St. George Hotel was considered a historic landmark. It was nestled in the mountain town of Canon City, Colorado right outside of the majestic Royal Gorge. It had a very colorful history, opening in 1876 as Colorado became the "Centennial State" and the railroad began to lay down the first tracks in the Gorge. Folks came from around the country seeking their fortunes with the railroad, prospecting or criss-crossing the west in search of land and a better life.

Helen stumbled across the St. George while driving through Canon City on her way to stay with her mother in Colorado Springs. She'd been on the road for over eight hours, the charming old hotel catching her eye as she drove through the main street of town in search of shelter for the night. The moment she walked into the place, she was instantly mesmerized. The night manager shared some of the hotel's history, famous people that had stayed there over the years, colorful anecdotes and ghost stories. Helen never went in for such things, any old building had a presence, it was unavoidable. You didn't need ghosts floating around in sheets to get the flavor of a place, it was in the bones and she had to admit, the St. George had some very unique bones.

The lobby was a sea of red, with overstuffed horsehair sofas and fainting couches. Gold accents adorned the walls, heavy velvet curtains with golden tassels hung in the beautiful beveled window panes. The wallpaper was restored and featured a red and gold raised fleur-de-lis pattern that felt soft and fuzzy to the touch. Here and there were ancient animal heads, deer, elk and bear, hanging proudly as if to proclaim that the hotel had not forgotten its western heritage. The ceiling was a work of art, hand-painted in a nature scene of the day leading to an old, golden caged elevator that looked like it would still need to be cranked by hand in order to operate.

Portraits of the various VIP guests throughout the decades covered the walls including a large painting of a little boy, hung over the stone fireplace. He had a mischievous smile, was wearing short pants and one of those "newsboy" caps at a jaunty angle on his bright blond head. He had a slingshot in one pocket and held a handful of marbles out in front of him, boastfully showing them off to her through the mists of time, nearly a century and a half ago. The artist had managed to capture him perfectly: a smudge of dirt on one cheek, a smattering of freckles across his nose and bright blue eyes. Helen felt a lump rise in her throat as she studied the painting, reluctantly turning away as the manager moved her along to show her the next bit of history.

The St. George was simply magical, like stepping back in time and for some unknown reason, it felt safe. It was a place that she could rest and regain her strength before facing her new life, one that she was in no hurry to begin. She immediately booked the "Teddy Roosevelt" room on the third floor, confident that this was the sanctuary she was so desperately craving.

Helen was an only child and her father had died some years ago, so her mother was really the only immediate family she had left, aside from her husband. Michael had come from a big family with four brothers so they never lacked for relatives on his side. Holidays with his family were loud and boisterous, the brothers roughhousing and laughing late into the night, their love for each other apparent. Helen wanted that for her own family, wanted so badly to be able to give that to Michael.

She and her mother were close, speaking every other day, but the distance between them grew wider as the years went on. She had gone away to law school the day after high school graduation, leaving her Colorado home behind and never looking back.

She and Michael moved quite a lot as each new career opportunity arose, both of them very driven, enjoying an active, fast-paced lifestyle. Going back to her mother now made her feel like an utter failure. With all of her success and accolades, she couldn't accomplish what the female half of the human race had been doing since the beginning of time. It was a bitter irony of course, since failure was the one thing Helen never envisioned for herself.

She spent her days sleeping in, something she never would have had time to do before. In the mornings she would have a quiet cup of coffee in her room, looking out of the window onto the quaint street below, picturing herself doing the exact same thing one-hundred-forty years ago. Her days were filled with wandering the local shops and sites around town. She even made a quick trip to the Colorado Prison Museum; Canon City and the surrounding areas contained at least thirteen high-security prisons including the infamous "Supermax Prison," home to the most dangerous inmates in the country.

She took long walks from one end of the town to the other, spending the bulk of her time in the cemetery searching the dates on the headstones, letting the familiar sadness fill her at each child's grave. *My baby will never have a grave like this, no one to mourn him, only me.*

On her third day at the hotel, the manager brought Helen into a special room, a library of old books that covered the entire wall in a giant oak-paneled bookshelf. Helen ran her hands along the dusty spines in awe, happier than she'd been in months. Books from every era of the St. George were displayed, all in varying states and conditions. He let her use the library every day, Helen spending hours there reading or in quiet reflection, finding an overstuffed chair with a patch of sunlight over in the corner. It was there that she met him for the first time, finding an old leather-bound journal sticking out at the end of the highest shelf. The pages were yellowed and brittle but she could still make out the words, the faded ink written in a child's sprawling hand.

"*Willie. I am Willie. Willie Willie Willie Willie!*" Helen smiled to herself as she turned each page of the journal, the little boy Willie leaping out at her from the page.

"*Momma said I oughtn't ever run inside, that little boys should be seen and never, ever heard. I oughtn't shoot my marbles in the halls or hide from the guests or slide down the banister faster'n any little boy in recorded history!! Momma works in the hotel*

*all day long now since Poppa went and got ~~blowed~~ blown up in
the tunnel. He was a railroad man, Poppa was. I was gonna be
a railroad man too, but now I have to be the man of the family,
Momma told me it was so.*

*Evr'y Sunday we visit him in the boneyard, Momma is very
sad, she always holds my hand. Momma said I am her lucky penny
'cause Colorado is shiny and new and I will grow up right along
with a brand new state! It's just the two of us now, Momma and
Willie agin the world."*

She looked up from the old journal, feeling the boy all
around her in this place. *Did he play hide and seek in here, in
this very room?* She could picture him in her mind, all elbows
and knees with a slightly dirty face running up and down the
corridors at full speed.

*Running loudly through the hallways must be the prerogative
of children in any era, she thought wistfully. I seem to be having
that very same problem. Willie, how old were you? Eight, nine
years old maybe? That's too young to lose a father, at least I had
almost thirty years with mine.*

Helen jumped up out of her chair, dropping the leather
volume to the floor as a loud bang hit the library door with
the sound of footsteps running away, a child's high-pitched
laughter. Helen sighed and picked up the journal, placing it
in her pocket. She would be sure to return it to the library as
soon as she was finished with it. In the meantime, she was
going to talk to the manager, this continued unruly behavior
was simply unacceptable.

"Children, ma'am?" the manager asked, confusion clouding his
face. "Why no, I don't believe so. There was a family with a

couple of girls here awhile back, two, maybe three weeks ago, but no boys that I can recall."

Helen tried to rein in her frustration. The manager was slightly disheveled, solidly middle- aged with a large, protruding potbelly. His handlebar mustache was old-fashioned and way too large for his face. Helen tried not to stare at it whenever she had a conversation with him, but today it was a losing battle. He was insistent that no young children were in the hotel. In fact, she had the entire third floor to herself right now, business at the hotel being extremely slow in the off- months. She went back to her room and picked up the journal, right where she left off.

"I have 10 Cats Eyes, 4 Striped Indians, 6 Alleys and 2 Flints. The kind man in room 203 gave me 6 Cats Eyes today, his boy Ed and me played all day, I won. Willie the Marble King!"

"ABCDEFGHIJKLMNOPQRSTUVW…WILLIE WILLIE WILLIE WILLIE! Momma said I am to practice my writing every day, she will check my spelling in here so I must be careful. She give me this book to write in and told me I must be ~~deligent~~ diligint?Momma?? Anyways, I am to do it every day before shootin marbles"

"The awful man at the front desk chases me evr'y day. He is big'n fat and mean jes like an old Walrus. Last week he boxed my ears for playin in the gold cage, just cause I jumped out and sceered him when he was turnin the handle, his face all red and puffed out. The Walrus can never catch me, I am the very fastest boy in the world bar none!!"

Helen laughed out loud at that last part, thinking that Willie could just as easily be describing the present day manager of the St. George.

"Momma said I need to put g's on the end of things like shootin and gettin and such. See Momma? S-H-O-O-T-I-N-G!

Willie the wonder boy! May I have my marbles back now, please Momma?"

The sun began to set over the mountains as Helen set the journal down. She felt a physical longing to hold her son in her arms, to reach back through the years and hug this fatherless boy. How smart he was, what a handful! She wondered if her little boy would have grown up like Willie, running and playing and having all sorts of boyish adventures. Mud and marbles, skinned knees and freckles. "Snips and snails and puppy dog tails," how wonderful that would have been! She flipped on the antique floor lamp in the corner and read on.

"Momma said that today I must be very very good. That she needs to keep workin working here so's we can live and be Momma and Willie against (see Momma I fixed it!) the world. I am gonna go outside and search for wild Indians jest just as soon I as shoot this last game! The Walrus is on the warpath today, Momma said I must be diligint? And stay out of his way. He makes Momma nervus nervous. Always standing way too close to her. I will make her happy today cause she is the very very very very best Momma in the entire world, bar none, and she says I am her incorrig incorrigible little boy. Lucky jes just like a shiny penny. Right Momma?"

That was all there was, Helen flipping through the final blank pages with a sense of profound sadness. *What happened to Willie the wonder boy and his loving Momma?* She made a mental note to go in search of the distasteful manager before dinner to see if he had any more history to share with her, such as the fate of one incorrigible, marble-shooting little boy from well over one hundred years ago. As she got ready to leave the room, she heard laughter, light and lyrical just outside of her door. As she opened it, the hallway was once again empty, but Helen was not surprised in the least. She was beginning to understand that the St. George was a very special place, more special than she could have ever imagined, in her wildest dreams.

Helen sat in the empty lobby, nursing a scotch on the rocks as she studied the painting of the little boy above the fireplace. The manager (or "Walrus II" as she thinks of him) didn't know who the little boy in the painting was or anything about Willie, but gave her a book to read called "The Most Haunted Places in Colorado." He was very proud of it, saying that the authors spent over two weeks at the St. George searching every nook and cranny for supernatural visitors. Apparently, the hotel was chock full of ghosts, Teddy Roosevelt had even made an appearance, but Helen had no interest in any of them, she only had eyes for one little boy.

She found him there on page 57, a hand-drawn picture of him that clearly matched the portrait in front of her. She read about the tale of a little boy named Willie whose mother worked as a maid for the St. George the year that it opened in 1876. She was widowed when the railroad team working the first tunnel in the Gorge were all killed in an explosion, the use of nitroglycerin for blowing through the mountains being very perilous in those days.

Willie lived an ideal existence at the hotel, running and playing while his mother toiled away. Tragically, he died at the bottom of the elegant staircase in the lobby after sliding down the banister at full speed, breaking his neck. It is said that the hotel manager was chasing him that day. Willie was always getting in trouble at the St. George, his exploits were legendary.

His mother died a year later, no cause was known but it was believed to be of a broken heart. They said that Willie roamed the hallways to this day in search of her, usually appearing to women or those who were suffering in some profound way.

Helen held up her glass in a silent toast to the painting before draining the scotch and getting up from her chair. This was Willie, it had to be. She could feel the pain of his mother, could relate to it for as awful as she felt about losing her own baby, she couldn't even imagine the magnitude of Momma's loss.

Her cell phone began to vibrate in her pocket. She picked it up and saw that Michael was calling. He'd left her three messages already along with a message from her mother, most likely wondering when she was coming home. She had been at the St. George for over a week now and was due at her mother's house days ago. She had no interest in calling either of them back right now, she had an errand she must run before it got too late.

When she reached her room, she gently placed a bag of brightly-colored marbles on the doorstep and went inside. She ran a hot bath and placed the items that she got at the local drugstore carefully on the sink. She had to really search to find marbles in the store, the clerk scouring every aisle of toys until he found some way in the back, hidden from view.

She opened the new bottle of scotch and poured three full fingers in the glass, washing down a couple of sleeping pills. She wanted to take the edge off, but still be alert enough when Willie finally came to her.

She smiled as she heard the footsteps approaching from down the hall and abruptly stop at her door. She heard him then, questioning though the door, "*Momma?*" She could hear the marbles moving as he picked them up and said again, more excitedly, "*Momma!*" *What a wonderful little boy, I can't wait to meet him.*

Helen went back into the bathroom, softly closing the door and slowly lowered herself into the antique bathtub. The water was almost scalding, felt purifying to her, cleansing her broken soul. She heard the front door open and shut, his footsteps stopping right outside of the bathroom door.

A light knocking, like birds' wings on the other side. Helen knew that he was impatient, but he'd waited so long already that a few more moments wouldn't make any difference. The lights in the bathroom began to flicker on and off as Helen thought of Michael and all that might have been. She felt the constant sadness of her lost babies, but also an excitement that there was a little boy who needed her right now, who would love her just as she was.

Helen was amazed there was no pain as she sliced the straight razor first over her left wrist, then her right. She watched the steady red flow in amazement. Blood had been the cause of her greatest despair and would now become her rebirth, she could hardly wait.

She began to get drowsy, her limbs all heavy and lethargic as the door opened and Willie stood at the threshold bathed in a bright light. As her vision slowly dimmed she saw his face, hopeful and happy as he glided towards the bathtub, marbles in his hand. He looked just like his painting, she thought in joy, my little boy! *Be patient, my lucky penny, I will be with you in just a moment.* It was her last conscious thought as the darkness enveloped her.

It would be Momma and Willie against the world. At long last.

Michael Wilson threw back his fourth scotch of the evening and stared blankly out of the window of the St. George Hotel. They had just buried his wife next to her father, Michael holding his mother-in-law's hand as she wailed in grief and pain next to the coffin of her only child. He was fraught with remorse and self-loathing, this was all his fault. He should never have left her, should have come home and dealt with his pain instead of running away.

He never got the chance to tell her that he wanted to try again, that they could work it all out somehow. He called her over and over, but Helen had never returned his calls. *What on earth was she doing in this place? Why had she chosen to end her life here?* Michael knew she was devastated about the miscarriages, but he never in a million years thought she would take her own life. *God, I loved her so much, how will I ever live without her?*

He drained the rest of the bottle, angry tears covering his face, completely lost in self-hatred and recrimination. He was on the third floor, about two rooms down from where they discovered his wife. They wouldn't give him the same room, it was locked up, unavailable to guests or the morbidly curious. Michael was trying to get a sense of what her last days were like, trying to reach out in his grief before saying goodbye.

A sudden tap on the door broke him out of his maudlin reverie, it was just past midnight, there should be no one at his door at this hour. Hours before he'd heard a child running up and down the hallway, thought nothing of it. Surely no children were still awake at this time? A second knock confirmed it, someone was definitely there.

"*Poppa?*" He heard, a child's voice unmistakably coming through the door, "*Poppa!*" Michael felt a slight chill run through him as he got up from the chair and went to open the door.

Originally published in "Under the Bed," December 2016

The Boys of Little Round Top

The smoke from the cannon blanketed the field in a dense, rolling fog that covered the prostrate bodies of the boys unlucky enough to draw the death card. He could see them lying there, impatiently still in their pretended demise, unable to check their cell phones or even post on Facebook.

James Lee wondered again what it must have really been like. The chaos and blood, the glory of dying for a lost cause, the nobility and perfect senselessness of it all. He was convinced that he was born into the wrong era, the crudeness and constant noise of modern times being extremely jarring for him. He crouched down and saw some of the boys in blue approaching. He did not want to get captured this time, would refuse to surrender without a fight or at least until he could get his part of the bar tab paid.

James hit the ground once more as the Union soldiers passed him by, his expensive, authentic butternut uniform grinding into the dirt and grime. He'd better not rip it—this one had cost him well over $400 to get every detail exactly correct, not to mention his gas and travel expenses just to get here. No, he would not, could not give up. The battle still had a long way to go and James had come a very, very long way to be here.

Grandma used to tell him that he had a connection to the great man himself. To about one eighth of one degree, but related all the same. His famous last name was a real badge of honor. James had always taken great pride in that small slice of his heritage, holding onto it in the sea of his mother's constant struggles to support them, his absent father's supreme indifference and the harsh realities of a so far, disappointing life.

Being born and bred on the southside of Chicago should have made him more partial to the Northern side of things, what with the "Land of Lincoln" and all, but his heart belonged to Dixie. He knew that in this day and age, honoring anything about the old South was frowned upon. Confederate flags were being removed, buildings renamed, history being scrubbed and judged by modern standards. The great evil of slavery was vanquished to the ash heap of history and good riddance as far as James was concerned. In that, he and Lincoln were in complete agreement.

No, the epic history-changing issues that fueled The War Between the States always felt above his pay grade, too political for his liking. Arguments from well over two hundred years ago to this very day were being endlessly debated and rehashed by far greater thinkers than himself and James was under no illusions that he would ever be included in such a distinguished group. What fueled his intense, almost obsessive interest in the War and all of its great battles was simply, the soldiers.

Ordinary men like himself, living their lives, barely scraping by, that were called to a cause, right or wrong. Something far greater than themselves, a higher purpose. For a brief shining time they became brothers in arms, willing to die to protect their way of life, their homes, their honor.

James knew that the vast majority of Confederate soldiers were dirt-poor farmers fighting against the low-wage factory workers and immigrants from up north. Nobodies from the lowest rung on the ladder of life went into battle with the likes of Generals Lee, Grant, Hancock, Longstreet or the doomed division of General Pickett, carving their names onto the rock of history for all time.

To James, nothing captured the adventure, romance and scale of the War more than one of its most legendary battles. Indeed, it was the pivotal battle that turned the tide, leading their fiery conflict to its inevitable end. The very name had always made his heart beat just a little faster, filling him with an inexplicable longing: Gettysburg.

James leapt up from his position, startling the Union soldiers and raising his Enfield Three-Band Percussion exact replica rifle (which set him back another hefty $250) directly at the Yank on the right. The black powder charge went off in a spectacular bang as he watched the man's surprised and disappointed face with a feeling of supreme satisfaction.

"Sorry Billy Yank, all's fair in love and war!" he said in his best imitation of a southern drawl, the unlucky man calling him a foul name before dropping to the ground in his pseudo-death. The other man scrambled away in an undignified, clumsy gallop. "Damned Polyester Soldier!" James called after him in disgust, hating the unserious, "weekend warrior" reenactors that populated these events.

James was a big believer in total immersion—he was strictly hardcore. When he took part in a reenactment, he was all in from the food he ate, weapons he used down to the shirt on his back. He even found an old locket with a tintype photograph of a woman he believed to be from the Civil War era at an antique store and kept her in his pocket, making up entire stories of their devoted, undying love.

He had been called a "stitch counter" before, a term that was meant to be an insult for Immersives like himself, but that he wore like a badge of honor. He may not be well educated, but he did know that polyester and hidden stitches weren't real common in the 1860s, and he was never afraid to point it out. He knew this hadn't made him many friends in the reenactment community, but it always gave him an intense burst of pride that he was getting as close as he possibly could to those heroic fighters from so long ago.

James sighed heavily as he watched the Yankee run off into the cannon smoke. It was only to be expected, he thought. This was the official reenactment on the 150th anniversary of Gettysburg and tons of "Mainstream" reenactors were here for the occasion. It was very special that they were even allowed on this hallowed ground, following in such brave footsteps on the very days the battle was fought. James swallowed his annoyance and remembered that he should be grateful, this was the defining experience of his young life.

When they were all done here, these guys would go back to the comfort of their own homes, surrounded by the miracles of modern technology. James would experience something akin to mourning when the battle had ended, an actual physical pain that he had to pull himself out of the nineteenth century and back into his everyday life.

In their tiny, rundown apartment on one of the many nights that his mother had to work the night shift, James came across "The Civil War" miniseries on TV. He was flipping through the channels in search of a cartoon when the grainy black and white footage with it's magical music filled the dark little room.

James was instantly transported, completely engrossed in what he saw. He watched it for hours until he could no longer keep his eyes open, his mother finding him face down in front of the TV when she got home, exhausted but changed forever. He found that he even knew some of the drills and routines of the soldiers, could feel their extreme discomfort on the long marches and heartbreak in their letters to home. More than once he knew the battle's outcome before the show told him about it, leaving his mother in astonishment that her nine-year-old son would know about such things. For his tenth birthday, she got him a collection of painted Civil War tin soldiers that he absolutely loved, even more so knowing how much it had cost her. When he turned twelve, she presented him with an old copy of the movie "Gettysburg" and the hook went in even deeper.

James was highly intelligent, but never did very well in school. Every chance he got, he would devour books about the Civil War, looking for every detail that he could possibly find about the lives of the soldiers. He decided that even though modern thought dictated that he shouldn't be, he was hopelessly attracted to the ill-fated plight of the Confederate man, like a moth to a flame.

He couldn't focus on anything else, barely managing to graduate from high school without ever having any kind of meaningful friendship or date. He tried studying history for a semester at the local Community College, but quickly grew restless. He wasn't sure what the future had in store, but he was certain that it would never be found in a class-room. History for him needed to be living and breathing, not a musty old footnote in some dry textbook. He began working odd jobs here and there, making just enough to move him along to the next place when he happened to see a notice in the local paper. He couldn't recall the name of the town anymore, but he most certainly remembered the ad. It was an open call for Civil War reenactors and on that day, his future was set.

Having dispatched the weekend warrior, James went off in search of his regiment, wandering as the smoke and fog thick-ened even more. He couldn't recall how he got separated from them, took out his antique compass and saw that the needle was circling furiously, like some sort of deranged stopwatch. He could feel the terrain change under his feet, becoming rockier with every step of his well-worn, hand sewn leather shoes. He sensed a change in the landscape, perhaps the be-ginning of a slight hill as the sound of a bugle horn blared off in the distance. He could feel a sudden electricity in the air as he climbed ever higher, and thought back to his knowledge of Gettysburg, remembering that Union officer John Buford had the incredible foresight to secure the high ground for the

North. That made all the difference, he thought, the South was finished before a single shot was ever fired.

A metallic smell assaulted his nose as goosebumps broke out all over his body. If he could only see where he was through this unearthly haze, maybe he could find his way back to his regiment. There were signs posted everywhere for tourists to find the various battle sites, surely he should be able to find one of them without leaving himself open to attack?

He began to feel weary, lightheaded as he continued up what was apparently a decent-sized hill. He needed to stop for a while, get his bearings before the daylight ran out. He had been here since dawn, choosing to set up his pup tent on the outskirts of the field where the event organizers had allowed the Immersives to camp. No comfy, modern motel for him, no way—he would have the full experience.

James searched for somewhere to sit for a moment, he literally couldn't even see his own hands in front of his face. Suddenly a sharp, zinging pain bit into his neck at full speed. *Damn it! What was that?* He felt an awful pinching sensation and slapped the area of his neck hard, convinced that one of those enormous mosquitoes that constantly plagued him in this ungodly July humidity had finally found its mark. Bug spray was not around for the Civil War soldier and so it wasn't included in James' provisions either. Rubbing his neck frantically, he saw there was blood on his hand, *that little bastard really got me, he thought, I hope I pulverized him good.*

James literally ran into a fairly large tree and sat down gratefully, uncapping his battered old canteen and taking a deep sip of the iron tasting water. *How did I get myself so lost? Maybe I'll just sit a spell and start out again in a few minutes.* His eyes began to feel heavy so he closed them for just an instant and dropped off into an uneasy doze.

A huge explosion from somewhere behind him made him jump to his feet, instantly awake and on his guard. The fog had cleared and he saw that he was at the bottom of a hill, "dead" rebel soldiers blanketing the terrain in a sickly gray hue. *Man, those guys are not going to be happy having to lay there in the hot sun for hours, he thought. I had better get moving.*

He broke out his one extravagance, a pair of actual bronze Civil War binoculars (another $250, thank you very much) and scanned the top of the hill. What he saw made him almost drop the binoculars in pure shock, a cold sweat breaking out on his brow. He could hardly believe it! Union soldiers were lining up at the top of the hill, taking orders from a man who he swore, must be General Joshua Lawrence Chamberlain of the 20th Maine Regiment.

Little Round Top! *Of course he thought in wonderment, it is July 2nd, this is Little Round Top. I can't believe my incredible good luck!* He thought back to all he knew of this decisive battle and remembered that Chamberlain was positioned on the very flank of the Union Army, there was no one past him—he was the absolute end of the line. If the Rebels were able to outflank him, they would gain the advantage and the Battle of Gettysburg might have had a very different outcome. He watched them line up in real time as he had seen over and over again in the movie and read about in countless books, the drama of this moment taking his breath away. He recalled that the 20th Maine was desperate, having fought off wave after wave of Confederates charging up the hill. They were running out of ammo, had precious few rounds left and the Rebs were gearing up for another try. He could hear commotion behind him, nervous voices, whispering and he knew that his brothers in arms were getting ready for that final, fateful charge.

God, he thought in awe, the man playing Chamberlain looks exactly like him—even more so than the actor from the movie. From the precise details of his uniform, down to the famous, walrus style mustache that he had seen in every single picture of the great man. Yankee though he was, James hugely admired him for his passionate convictions and undisputed bravery. Bravery that he, James Lee, would get to witness live and in person or at least, a very close approximation of it—this was shaping up to be the very best day of his life.

The 20th Maine fanned out into a long line, getting ready to charge down the hill in what James knew was called a right-wheel maneuver. He also knew that in just a few moments, Chamberlain would order a bayonet charge in a last ditch attempt to hold them off, their ammunition completely depleted. *Man these guys are spot on! This must have been exactly how it was, how fortunate am I to be here today!*

He could feel a great rumbling coming from behind, followed by a sound that raised the hair upon his head, bringing sudden tears to his eyes. It was a sound that he never dreamed he would hear, a sound that no one living could ever exactly reproduce. How on earth did these reenactors know how to pull off what must be an actual, real live Rebel Yell?

He remembered the part in "The Civil War" series where old grainy movie reels showed elderly Union and Confederate veterans shaking hands over a fence at Gettysburg. Impossibly old, especially in those days, the ancient warriors were asked to demonstrate the Rebel Yell, but were too feeble at that point to really do it justice. Not like this. This felt real, a little too real as he turned to face the onslaught of Rebel soldiers heading straight for him at a dead run.

He jumped back up and flattened himself against the tree, momentarily paralyzed by the otherworldliness of his situation. His head told him that this was just part of the weekend's events but his heart was telling him something else entirely. The men that streaked past him looked like no other reenactors he had ever seen. Not a single weekend warrior in the bunch. These men were impossibly lean, battle-scarred and almost feral. Their faces were stretched into terrifying masks as they screamed like banshees, determined and deadly. He swallowed hard and tasted the cold steel of fear in the back of his throat as he watched Chamberlain hold his sword high up into the air and bellow out the only word that could be heard above the roaring, hellish din "Bayonets!"

He heard the sound of Rebel ammunition landing all around him, an actual Minie Ball hitting the tree right above his head as he realized that these men were using live rounds in this battle. The 20th Maine dashed down the hill in a great whoosh, bayonets extended and James could see as if in slow motion, the clash that was about to come.

Before he could even form a rational thought, he ran out into the onslaught of Rebels, trying to warn them that the Yankees had no ammunition, this charge was all for show. He tried several times, yelling into the chaos until he was raspy and hoarse, but it was no use. The outcome of this battle had already been decided. 150 years ago on this very day. Right now.

Chamberlain's great gamble would pay off, the Confederates would retreat and surrender to men with no bullets in their guns and the South would follow the path to their own destruction in a blaze of futile glory. The war was a waste of such magnitude, such enormous loss of lives but, Oh! What a moment to be alive, what a fight!

He looked up and watched as the two sides met in bloody battle, the fierceness of the 20th Maine beginning to overcome his brethren, for they were desperate men with nothing in the world left to lose—defend the flank or die. It was everything he had ever expected and more, in all of its horror and bloodstained majesty. Tears ran openly down James' face as he saw the men begin to flicker and fade, like an old-time home movie. He could actually look through them, they were vapors in the mist and he knew that he might only have precious seconds before they were lost to him forever—these Boys of Little Round Top.

An impossibly thin man broke away from the charging pack and came right over to James, a smile lighting up his dirty, unshaven face. James felt an instant jolt of recognition—how did he know this man? He couldn't recall seeing him at any of the reenactor events but was absolutely certain that he knew him, had always known him.

"Where have you been old Jim?" he asked in a slow drawl, grabbing James by the shoulders in a brotherly embrace. "We've been waitin' for you!"

James looked on with disbelief as the man held out a battered old rifle, presenting it to James as a gift. James gently took hold of the stock, running his other hand along the barrel in a smooth, practiced motion. It felt like a long-lost friend, like coming home. They shook hands warmly and the man turned back to the battle, stopped, then held out his arm, inviting James to follow.

James took one final, slow breath as he stepped away from the tree. Behind him he saw his fellow reenactors in the distance, packing it in for the day, heading back to the comfort of their hotel rooms, Wi-fi and fast food. In front of him, the battle continued—Minie Balls whistling through the air, the clash of bayonets, screams and chaos. He knew what his decision would be in an instant, there never really was any doubt. He felt a moment of regret for his mother, hoped that she would be alright as he picked up his real rifle, leaning the expensive replica up against the tree like the husk of an old shell.

Old Jim stepped forward and followed his brother into battle, letting out a joyful, ear-splitting yell as he ran straight into his heart's desire, and into history.

Claire Lee stood at the bottom of Little Round Top, trying to feel what her son's last moments must have been like. She was cradling his replica rifle while holding a handful of brochures from the Gettysburg National Military Park. It was a complete fluke they told her, a horrible accident. Event planners were very meticulous when it came to firearm safety at these reenactments, checking each firearm with ramrods to ensure that no live rounds remained within.

Unfortunately, one well-meaning inspector got distracted and left his ramrod in a reenactor's weapon, turning it into a projectile when fired with black powder. James never had a chance, getting shot in the side of his neck with deadly force by the ramrod and bleeding out before the EMTs could get to him. Horribly, the ramrod passed completely through James' neck, landing in the tree next to his propped up rifle like a bloody arrow.

Nobody could tell her how he had wandered off so far from his assigned regiment or how the poor, distraught Union reenactor came upon him all the way out at Little Round Top, killing him in an instant without meaning to. It wouldn't have mattered anyway, Claire knew her son. He was exactly where he wanted to be.

She'd spent years working two to three jobs at a time, desperately trying to support them after his father ran out. She had spent so much time trying to eke out a living that she lost him somewhere along the way, she thought sadly. Lost him to another place, another time. Lost him to history.

The officials were very very sympathetic of course, everyone signed waivers at these events, there was always an element of risk involved. They even allowed her to sprinkle James' ashes on the hill of Little Round Top, right by the tree where they'd found his rifle. Claire was devastated, but at least she had the small comfort that James died doing what he loved, what he truly believed he was born to do.

She felt the tears coming again and bitterly wiped them away with the back of her hand. She reached into her purse to grab a Kleenex, dropping the brochures onto the ground. As she bent down to pick them up, she saw a picture on the top brochure staring out at her and felt an electric shock, adrenaline instantly coursing through her body. The Kleenex forgotten, Claire sat down heavily on the ground, allowing the tears to stream down her face as she stared into the face of her only child, her son.

He was there in an old black and white picture dated 1863, his clean-shaven, eager face beaming up at her as he posed with his regiment in full Confederate regalia. There were no names, just a date and a simple caption. Claire knew without a single doubt, that this was James, as she rocked back and forth in the dirt, holding herself and laughing uncontrollably through her tears.

He was happy. She could see it in his eyes, at long last, he was truly happy. Claire picked herself up and said goodbye to her only boy, taking a final look at the hill where he was resting. She held the brochure close to her heart as she walked back through the Park, the caption of the old tintype photo running over and over through her mind, now etched forever on her heart:

"The Boys of Little Round Top."

Originally published in "Bewildering Stories," 2016

Furry Children

The dog and the cat were seldom in agreement, that was just a given. There were very few times over the course of an average year when they would actually work together for the greater good. Like when food was dropped onto the floor or the back door left open just a crack, allowing them a brief taste of mutual freedom. In times like that, Marie would always hold back, giving them a quick moment to savor their victory before intervening in any given situation. She wanted them to be a team, for that is what they were. Dog, cat, human, all starting out a new chapter in life—the three of them against the world.

Now she watched as they sat, side by side, heads swiveling in perfect synchronicity, clearly fascinated by something that Marie couldn't see. She turned, suddenly, to look behind her, feeling more than a little ridiculous. Perhaps a stray bug had somehow gotten in, a loose floating string or an errant beam of sunshine? Nothing. Total silence.

Marie shook her head and turned back to watch them. She saw, in complete wonderment their fascinated expressions, both feline and canine. She calmly tried to tamp down the sudden chill that tickled the base of her spine. *It's only the beginning, way too early to be cracking up, she thought sadly. He has only been gone for two weeks, I need to keep it together.*

Marie couldn't recall the exact moment when her marriage began to unravel, but remembered it was pretty anti-climatic. A mutual exhaustion after trying too hard for over twenty years, with a dash of infidelity thrown in for good measure. She was loathe to admit it, but they were the typical middle-aged couple, slowly growing apart as their waistlines grew out. The spark was still there, but neither one of them cared to look for it anymore, or remembered how it all began in the first place.

John, of course, just had to have the typical mid-life crisis, trading her in for a younger model—that stupid, overused cliche in the flesh. A new fling, she assumed, who would give him children since Marie never could. Not for lack of trying, but it seemed that Marie was the problem. She was barren. Or whatever the cold, impartial medical term was for it these days. Marie had made her peace with it long ago, letting her "furry children" fill the painful void in her heart, but it would seem, that Johnny had not.

They'd gone through several sets of pets throughout the years, living a comfortable life together, such as it was, or so she had thought. The day he left, he talked about taking the animals with him, but Marie wouldn't relent. She would never give them up. They had only been in the new house for about a year and there were too many other things to fight over. Bills, mortgage, mistress and a thousand other things that made Marie want to dive under the covers in complete despair. He could walk out on her, on their marriage, but he would never take them. Never.

The dog eagerly wagged his tail almost in greeting as the cat rubbed her face against the dog's front leg, purring loudly. Marie looked around the room again, trying to figure out what had them acting so strangely. The real estate agent told them when they bought the house that something bad had happened here. Marie didn't want to know anything about it, but Johnny had looked into it, something about a murder-suicide. They'd gotten such a good deal on the house that Marie refused to entertain the notion of a haunting, that stuff was pure nonsense as far as she was concerned. Now, with her animals acting this way, she wondered if maybe there was something to it after all. Hadn't she heard somewhere that pets could see things that their owners could not?

"Hello?" she said out loud to the empty room, "Is there anybody here?"

As if in response, a late autumn breeze lifted the curtains around the open window, making Marie jump a little.

That's all it is, she thought in relief. No ghosts, just a passing distraction outside, they'll calm down in a minute or two.

The dog let out a sudden bark making Marie nearly leap out of her skin. He walked right past her and sat down heavily, making a small whining noise. The cat jumped down from her perch and joined him there, both of them looking up in anticipation. She heard it then, a slight noise behind her. Some sort of shifting as Marie felt a sudden jolt of adrenaline, her heart slamming against her chest.

Johnny told her in the garden, while both of her hands were buried deep in the wet earth. Marie was very proud of her garden, she'd started out as an Iowa farm girl and had managed to keep that part of her identity even living out here in the wilds of suburbia.

He was in love he said, he hadn't planned for it to happen but it had. She needed to let him go. She remembered standing up and grabbing the shovel, turning the dirt over and over while he stood pleading with her, insisting that he no longer loved her, that their marriage was finished. They would both be better off he told her, this had been coming for a long time—it was time to be honest about it. She couldn't remember a thing after that, just the endless digging and turning of her beloved soil until she could no longer hear him.

Now she stood crying in her shower, great heaving sobs of misery that he would betray her this way, that he would break his vows. The steam and hot water were washing her body clean, but were not able to cleanse her broken heart, her shattered soul.

The dog came into the bathroom, alerted like he always was when Marie was upset. She turned the water off and opened the glass door, noticing that he had a large object in his mouth. He loved to play "keep away" with her, waggling his entire back end and playfully growling as Marie fumbled, trying in vain to grab it from his mouth. The dog was covered in dirt, with what she assumed was topsoil from her garden. A foul smell assaulted her as she reached out in a panic and managed to get a hold of it.

A hunk of blackened, rotting flesh came off in her hand as the dog pulled the severed arm away, enjoying their little game as usual. He turned and dashed away, forcing Marie to run through the house completely naked to chase him down. She caught him near the compost pile in her garden, the dog reveling in his newfound treasure. Pieces of dismembered corpse were strewn across her tomato patch and onto the lawn like a gruesome crop ready for harvest. Marie picked up her battered old shovel and went to work reburying her faithless husband.

Marie knew without looking that she was no longer alone, but then again, she always could sense when he was near and had for over twenty years. A hot, rancid breath hit the back of her neck as the cat and dog pranced and leaped all around her, delighted in their supernatural reunion.

"Honey, I'm home," Johnny croaked into her ear, fresh earth plopping onto the floor as his one good arm snaked around her shoulders, "I'll never leave you again."

Marie didn't know what to expect when she finally turned around, but she knew one thing for certain. Johnny was finally honoring his vows and "til death do us part" was about to take on a whole new meaning.

Originally published in "Friday Fiction," 2016 and reprinted in "Dark Fire Fiction," 2017

The Resurrectionist

The skull sat in all of its Shakespearean glory on the antique desk, shiny and proud. A long fracture ran down the back of it like a seam, almost rendering the skull in two. The crack was so perfectly placed, so well done, that he actually got emotional when he gazed upon it, admiring the craftsmanship. Whoever caused its demise had certainly left an indelible mark, the work of a true professional.

The skull was the first thing that greeted him each morning and the last thing he checked before turning in. He was consumed with curiosity and would sit contemplating it for hours, wondering what sort of "skulduggery" had come upon it. He would often chuckle at the pun, for he was a witty fellow, he really was. It was one of his most admirable qualities.

He'd grown up fast and hard on the streets, one of the many unwashed masses in the worst part of the slums. He'd had to resort to all sorts of chicanery over the years, becoming lean and deadly as a result. He grew up tall and cadaverous, never knowing a full meal in his short, brutish life. He had fought and clawed his way up in order to survive many times over, even killing when he'd had to. He'd stolen, begged and done a myriad of unmentionable, soul-crushing things with nothing but a long, jagged scar covering his left cheek to show for it.

Some years back, he'd fallen in with a gang who introduced him to his current and most lucrative profession. He became the top man in his field, eventually usurping his original partners, although there was still a bit of controversy over their sudden disappearance. He'd built a solid network and was the most sought after supplier of his trade, the very pinnacle of success. In time, he became known by his appearance and ghoulish demeanor, his long skull-like face the perfect embodiment of his life's chosen path. They called him the Cadaver and everyone marveled at his talent for the harvesting and delivering of fresh corpses, paying him handsomely for services rendered.

They were known as resurrectionists. Both feared and reviled, they were a necessary evil in a profession desperately seeking hands-on knowledge. A good resurrectionist was worth his weight in gold to the hospitals and anatomical schools in the city. Bodies were commodities, there being only so many executions a year. A precious few were legally allowed for study and that is precisely where the Cadaver and his associates would come in. He could secure anywhere from eight to fourteen guineas for a complete corpse, depending on the state of decrepitude. Fresher was always for the better, of course. Lesser amounts would be collected for infants, children or various and sundry parts. The Cadaver knew how to extract his wares with exquisite care, he was thorough and careful, demanding the same level of excellence from each of his many crews.

On the night the skull appeared, in a rare episode of carelessness he'd almost gotten caught. He was hip-deep in a freshly turned grave when a flash of white caught his eye in the blackened night. It was placed in the dirt some two feet above the coffin, quite unexpected and on its own. He reached down and cradled it in his arm, feeling an instant connection to the morbid object.

The skull stared up at him, defiance oozing out of its empty sockets. The Cadaver was entranced, puzzled as to the location of the body that belonged to it for the skull was quite alone. He picked it up, holding it lovingly in his hands, turning it this way and that, examining the deadly, precise fracture running up along its back. He was so mesmerized by the skull that he failed to hear the night guard making his rounds, the man's lantern cutting through the darkness.

The Cadaver had dealt with this particular guard on a regular basis, knew his habits well. The families of the dearly departed had pooled their resources in order to protect their loved ones from the anatomist's knife and men such as himself. This guard was definitely not worth their recompense. He was corpulent, slowed by drink and overindulgence. He was no match for the Cadaver on a regular night, but this night was turning out to be exceptional indeed.

As the guard approached, he sprang into the open grave, lying as still as a corpse on top of the simple wooden coffin within, the skull still grasped in his long, bony fingers. He could hear the guard lumbering above, his drunken out-of-tune whistling informing the Cadaver that the man was indeed, well into his cups again.

With the stillness of death, the Cadaver straddled the object of his exertions, waiting for a full five minutes after the guard passed by. In what he could only describe as a miracle, he had not been discovered. He hurried to capitalize on his good fortune. After removing her wedding ring, he quickly extricated the newly-dead woman. She had died young, in child bed he deduced, after finding the body of a small babe tucked in next to her. That was a bonus. Both of them would fetch him a tidy sum but he needed to act quickly before true decay set in. He rolled them onto his tarp, gently heaving the bodies over his shoulder to where his hidden cart awaited. On impulse, he grabbed the skull and shoved it in his bag before making his getaway into the foggy night.

Since that evening, he'd been obsessed with the skull—its mystery—who it had been and why it was buried alone. He'd been in such a hurried state that he really hadn't had the time to investigate more thoroughly. He didn't venture out in the field too much anymore, he had several crews that would scour the cemeteries at night digging up fresh bodies and delivering the Cadaver his cut at the end of each shift. He was infamous in their tight-knit community and had many enemies waiting to take him down, so he was always extremely careful.

This night, he thought he would take a chance and go back to where he'd found the skull. Maybe there was some detail he missed, some clue to its origins. He felt confident in his own ability to get in and out quietly and quickly, no one the wiser that he had ever been there. Sometimes a man had to get his hands dirty and go back to his roots, he thought as he packed up his tools for the evening. If he was lucky, he might come across a new body as well. There had been a rash of consumption deaths recently. A good resurrectionist always kept up on all the local news, he read it all. He gave the skull a final look on his way out of the door, caressing its smooth surface before bidding it a fond farewell for the evening.

The Cadaver hid his cart in the usual spot and walked softly past the guard who was sound asleep at his post. There should be no trouble this night. He quickly moved past Potter's Field. The long freshly-replenished trench was usually a prime spot for a resurrectionist, but the Cadaver was on a special errand this night. He made his way over to the quadrant where he'd found his skeletal companion and laid out the tools of his trade. The grave had been filled in, of course, the first shootings of green appearing on top of the packed-in mound. The Cadaver went to work, attacking the earth with relish, his passion for his livelihood apparent in every shovelful. When he had dug down to where the skull had been discovered, he sifted through the wet earth with has hands, searching for any hint or artifact. Where was the body? he asked himself for perhaps the one-hundredth time, remembering that the skull had been alone when he'd come upon it.

Down and down he dug, his spidery arms aching with the effort. A sudden gleam caught his weary eye as he quickly scrabbled for the item, holding it up to his face in triumph. The clouds had just moved past the full moon allowing the Cadaver to get a clear look at his prize. He held it up by the golden chain, allowing the timepiece to swing gently in the night. It was a pocket watch made of gold, his first real extravagance after he'd begun to build up his trade. It had never left his person since he first purchased it some ten years ago.

He frantically patted his pocket, searching in vain, for there was nothing there. His prized possession sat in his hands moments after he had just dug it out of a six-foot grave. This was simply not possible since he knew he'd just pulled the timepiece from his own pocket, not an hour before to wind it. It was caked in dried mud and grime and the Cadaver only had precious seconds to wonder at the strangeness of his situation before an ax slashed through the blackness of the night, nearly cleaving his head in two.

It struck him in the back of his head in a perfect line, the bearer of the fatal blow sticking his foot into the Cadaver's back and roughly yanking the ax out before delivering the coup de grace. The rival resurrectionist lifted the bloody ax high into the air and cleanly lopped off the Cadaver's battered head in one swift strike. He always made sure to keep his ax sharpened, for you never knew when it would be needed to break into an intractable coffin or to thwart an enemy, just like tonight.

It was quite a prize for the man, for the Cadaver had been very careful never to get caught in his long and distinguished career, especially by any rivals in the field. It seemed the famed resurrectionist's luck had finally run out, the man thought as he kicked the severed head back into the open grave and carefully rolled what was left of his kill onto a tarp. The body, even without its head, would fetch him a good sum. There was no need for this night to be completely wasted, the Cadaver of all people would have understood that.

Never one to leave a site in disarray, the attacker quickly buried the head with the overturned earth and hastily tamped it down. Satisfied that things appeared to be in order, he loaded up his cart and rode straight to the anatomy theatre. He was careful, lest he leave too much of a trail in his wake for there was quite a lot of blood left in the decapitated remains of the Cadaver. Once the body was safely deposited, he would have more than enough for an evening at the pub, perhaps even with Ruthie at his side if she wasn't otherwise engaged for the evening.

The disappearance of the Cadaver was the talk of their profession for awhile, but resurrectionists were a notoriously closed-off lot. Nobody really wanted to delve into the mystery too closely. After all, there would be a new boss soon, shooting up like a weed in Potter's Field. Better not to create any acrimony.

As for the Cadaver, his head remained safely tucked away in the earth awaiting discovery, whilst his body became a true cadaver at long last. He was fodder for the study of young anatomists, his organs poked and prodded, mapped, charted and picked apart by a dozen eager hands.

Oh, how he would have appreciated the irony.

Originally published in "Pilcrow&Dagger," August/September 2017 and "Weird Reader" 2017 Edition

Sourdough's Cabin

Sourdough

The snow blanketed the land in every direction, the towering pine and aspen trees keeping watch over the mountain like sentinels in a storm.

Ol' Sourdough rubbed the sleep from his eyes, getting up from the warm pallet as his old bones creaked and popped. He had been alive for a long, long time and seen many a storm. This one here was a good'n. He knew that his shelter was completely buried, but for the first time in days, the whistling and groaning of the winter wind had mercifully stopped. The silence was deafening as Sourdough broke through the top layer of ice in his water bin and quickly wet his lips. He would have some work to do today if he was to have any hope of seeing the sun again.

As soon as he was growed enough, Sourdough lit out for the West, spending years traversing the hills and streams of fur country in the Shining Mountains, otherwise known as the Rockies. He had been a free trapper, trader, prospector and guide, helping many a tenderfoot navigate their way across the mountain passes and rugged trails that crisscrossed the land. He never stayed in one place very long, and had no family laying claim on him. Sourdough was totally alone, or as he thought of it, living the life of a free man. He traveled with an old mule he named Sara (after a long-lost love) that helped him lug the timber up and down the mule trails of Santa Fe mountain, the railroad paying him for each load they delivered. He and Sara traipsed up and down the mountain in fine fettle until the first leaves turned. Then that old girl laid down and died, having lived a good life of service to him. Sourdough was not the sentimental sort, but he was getting up there in years and decided to settle down on the spot where he had buried his old friend, just to wait out the winter.

Sourdough reached into his possibles bag and fetched his pipe and the very last of the tobacco he had traded for last summer out at Bent's Old Fort, before he and Sara headed up into the hills. He took a long, satisfying pull on the pipe and threw a handful of kindling onto the small fire.

The smoke hole was holding up pretty well, he thought. The heat was melting the snow around the hole, keeping the place warm while the snow and winds raged outside. With the pemmican and the few food items he still had stored away, Sourdough knew that he could last a lot longer in here but was beginning to feel the itch, knowing that many a mountain man had gone under after being stuck in one place for too long. It was known as "seeing the elephant," that giant, monstrous beast of a vision that made many a free man lose his wits and will to survive.

That was one old gal Sourdough had no intention of meeting. He closed one eye and peered up the smoke hole, looking for the sun and praying that he would find it shining through. He could see a small sliver of bright light and knew that this was it, his golden opportunity.

CJ

Charles James, affectionately known to his family and friends as CJ, was on a bit of an adventure. He had been slightly adrift, having recently graduated from high school, spending all summer working with his hands at any job he could possibly get that would keep him outdoors and moving. He wasn't sure exactly what he wanted to do with his life, just that he was impatient for it to actually begin. He always had what his mother called "the wanderlust," a desire to see what lies over the next hill, down the farthest path or better yet, off of it. His parents nagged at him constantly to choose a college or career, but CJ held out, saving his money and getting stronger from the physical demands of each new job, closing his eyes every night with the satisfaction of a hard day's work well done.

His cell phone chirped out a warning to him that he was getting low on juice; the charger in his old red Ford pickup wasn't the greatest. It was a crisp, winter Colorado morning and CJ was determined to get out at first light. The weather was unusually warm this year, leaving him with the perfect opportunity to accomplish his goal. His constant companion, a young Golden Retriever named Cassie, sat beside him, joyfully sticking her head out of the window into the thin mountain air as they rounded the bend and the old mining town of Idaho Springs loomed into their view.

His father had taken him up here for as long as he could remember. They owned eighty acres on North Santa Fe mountain and almost every year without fail, CJ and his dad would brave the rugged, rocky dirt road that was only accessible by a four-wheel drive to go and pick out the perfect Christmas tree. They would make a great adventure out of it, hiking through the thick woods, making sure they found the very best one that would make his mother and sisters laugh with delight. Once they found it, Dad would reverently take his hand and they would both touch the trunk of the tree, gauging its size and exactly which tools they would need.

By the time he was ten, CJ could wield the ax like a pro, Dad always watching with a sharp eye to make sure he was being safe. Once the tree was down, they would gently pack it up, stopping for a picnic lunch somewhere along the way, drinking in the magnificent sights and sounds of nature all around them. CJ had spent years of his young life camping, hiking, and wandering the great outdoors, but the time spent on Santa Fe mountain with his father was special. The conversations they would have, the skills his father would teach him and always, there was the mountain, the one place where CJ felt his heart swell with freedom and joy. His father would regale him with stories of the hearty trappers and mountain men that had actually lived on the mountain and more than once CJ would close his eyes and imagine what that must have been like, wishing more than anything that he could be one of them.

Cassie let out a sharp bark as CJ rounded the bend to where the paved road stopped and the dirt one began. It was a long, treacherous climb up the mountain and CJ laughed as he remembered his mother and sisters covering their eyes on the way up, afraid to look straight down into the abyss. There wasn't a single guardrail in sight. CJ loved it, craning his head as far out of the window as Dad would allow while Mom watched him nervously through her fingers.

"Well, this is it, girl. Are you ready?" he said to Cassie as he stopped the truck and put it into four-wheel drive, excited as he always was, to get back up to his beloved mountain.

Sourdough

Sourdough spent the better part of the morning digging himself out. Using his old pickaxe, he hammered away relentlessly at the wall of snow and ice, inch by inch, until the first rays of the sun beamed down upon his his grizzled old face. By midday, he had just about cleared the doorway and was able to take his first step into the outside world in over a week. The sun was blinding as Sourdough took a moment to acclimate himself, feeling the crisp, thin mountain air on his face. It was a white, shining paradise all around him in every direction, and Sourdough thought that if this wasn't Heaven, it was the closest thing to it. As always, he thanked the Man On High for making him the luckiest and freest creature on the face of this old earth: a mountain man.

He turned to survey his handiwork. The cabin had held up remarkably well, he thought with pride. He and Sara had lugged enough lumber up and down the trail for him to keep a few logs. He worked away all summer into the fall, his mule keeping him company until she left him and the skeleton of his cabin was completed. He had just laid down the roof and filled all the gaps with mud when the first snows began, ending in an epic, swirling storm that kept him holed up for nearly a week. Crude though it was, Sourdough had to admit that it was the finest home he could recall, having lived under the stars for the better part of forty years.

It would be a real shame to leave it in the spring, he thought——maybe I'll stay a spell. He could certainly still set his traps, although every year he had to climb higher and higher to find beavers. Before long there wouldn't be any of the little critters left.

Sourdough pointed his makeshift snowshoes downward and began the long trek. With his old Hawken muzzle-loading rifle slung over his back, he slowly made his way through the snow in search of provisions. He didn't expect he'd find a buck, but a nice tasty squirrel was a real possibility. Sourdough could see that the afternoon was beginning to turn dark again, snow clouds getting ready for another go——he had better be quick. He'd gone on for a long while when he noticed that the snow was completely melted from the ground. He stopped and looked back. Behind him, there was a foot or more, the prints from his snowshoes staring back at him defiantly. Here, where he was standing, there was nothing. It was like the storm had never happened. He was about to turn back to investigate when a sudden sound startled him, unlike anything he had ever heard before, piercing the still afternoon air. A rumbling, menacing sound.

A train engine? No that's not possible; there are no trains anywhere near the mountain. Sourdough flattened himself against the trunk of a large aspen and waited. He had managed to keep his topknot for nigh on seventy years now, despite almost getting scalped by a Pawnee brave some years back. He didn't get to be this advanced age by being careless.

A sudden mist sprung up out of the ground, putting him instantly on guard. Something strange was afoot, all of his senses were on fire. Out of the spidery haze an astonishing vision barreled into his line of sight, roaring past him as Sourdough clutched his rifle in abject terror.

What manner of creature is this? He desperately tried to make sense out of his predicament as the strange monster came to a stop just yards below him. It was enormous, made of some kind of iron, garishly red and demonic with smoke bellowing from its underbelly. Sourdough aimed his Hawken straight at it then nearly fainted dead away as it opened itself up and a man with a big golden dog stepped out. Both were wearing some unearthly shade of orange and Sourdough pondered that he must have fallen into Hell. All of this simply could not be real.

CJ

CJ checked to make sure Cassie's optic-orange vest was secure. There were always hunters on Santa Fe mountain and he didn't want his dog mistaken for a deer, or himself for that matter. He made sure he had everything he needed—tools, ax, knife, bear spray. He had never heard of bears being on the mountain before, but he was very careful about his surroundings. He always took precautions, knowing the mountain can turn on you in a heartbeat. He packed up the last of his provisions, making sure there was enough food and water for the day and turned to look at the mountain.

He was feeling a little distant from his family these days. His father had been too busy with work and couldn't make it up to the mountain this year. CJ was the youngest of three and his sisters were both in college. There really was no time or reason to keep up their annual Christmas tradition; no one was expecting it. CJ felt that bringing back the perfect Christmas tree would be a special gift to them, his way of showing his appreciation.

He also wanted to prove that he was finally responsible enough to carry on the tradition all on his own, for he had no doubt that someday he would bring his own children up to the mountain. If he could find a way, perhaps he would even make the mountain his permanent home.

CJ felt a slight change in the air as a light mist began to gather around his feet. The morning had been clear, but clouds were starting to gather off in the distance. He whistled to Cassie and found her completely still, locked onto something about halfway up the first hill. A light growl escaped her throat, a sound he knew all too well, especially when there was a squirrel anywhere nearby. He looked up to see why she was staring so intently. Nothing. Complete stillness.

He got a sudden sensation that he was being watched as his hand instinctively reached for the large hunting knife on his hip.

"Hello? Is there anyone there?" Cassie barked once, breaking him out of his reverie. She ran up to him, tail wagging in anticipation. The feeling passed and CJ guessed that whatever it was had gone. He started up the mountain with Cassie running ahead in excitement. He remembered a certain clearing with a large copse of pine trees about a half-mile up. He would find his tree there. Man and dog made their way up the mountain as the feathery mist continued to grow and billow out behind them, the first snowflakes falling gently to the earth.

Sourdough

Sourdough deftly followed the man and dog as they made their way up the north side of the mountain. He was an expert tracker, but he had to admit that the dog almost flushed him out, he needed to watch his every move. He could see that the man was young, little more than a boy. He was still beardless, with short yellow hair, carrying a large satchel on his back. He wore strange clothing, including a painfully-bright orange garment of a shade Sourdough had never seen before, perfectly matching the one on his long-haired dog. They made quite a pair as they lumbered their way up to the clearing ahead. The boy seemed to know his way around the mountain, but he wouldn't keep his hair on his head very long if the Ute were tracking him. They would hear him coming a mile away.

Sourdough looked up and saw the most peculiar thing—the sky appeared to be bending, moving and shimmering in a way he couldn't fathom. He felt a sudden pressure in his head, a ringing in his ears and saw the boy and dog begin to flicker, like flames.

What is tarnation is going on? They made the clearing and the boy stopped in front of a decent-sized pine tree, circled around and looked at it from every direction. He said something to the dog *(Cassie? Is that what he called her?)* and pulled an ax from his sack. The boy laid his hand on the trunk of the tree in some sort of ritual then backed away and took his first swing. Sourdough had to admit that the boy was pretty handy with an ax as he watched him bring down the tree, then expertly truss it up and harness it onto his back.

Now why did he choose that particular tree out of all the ones along the way? The boy checked to make sure the harness was secure then took the whole thing off and proceeded to throw a stick for the dog laughing in pure delight as she nearly knocked him over. Sourdough held back a chuckle, feeling the camaraderie of man and beast. Just like how he and old Sara used to be. Lord, how he missed that old mule!

He continued to watch as they played, then settled in for a midday meal on the stump of a tree, the boy throwing scraps of meat to his over-eager dog. Sourdough grabbed some pemmican from his bag and took a bite, keeping a close watch on the pair as the odd, rippling sky suddenly opened up and the snow began to come down in waves.

CJ

CJ knew it was the one as soon as they hit the clearing. It stood apart from the others, proud and perfectly formed. He placed his hand gently on its trunk in the well-loved tradition, a hundred memories hitting him all at once.

He could picture the tree in their front window, decorated with all of his mother's favorite ornaments. She always had to get an ornament at every single family trip or event— they took up the entire tree. Bing Crosby would be singing in the background as he and his sisters looped string after string of lights around the tree, laughing at their Mom's self-proclaimed, tacky decorating style. Everyone at home for the holidays, all of them together.

CJ had prepared a travois that he planned to harness to his back in order to bring the tree down the mountain, just as his father had taught him. The weather seemed to be holding out, he figured they had time for lunch and a quick round of fetch before heading back to the truck. A movement in the sky caught his eye and he looked up into an incredible sight.

The sky was filled with colors, like a wavy, psychedelic Aurora Borealis. CJ stood up, feeling lightheaded as he watched the sky tumble and churn. A random jumble of high-pitched sounds hit him all at once, making his head spin. He jumped up in alarm, calling Cassie to him and quickly gathered up his gear to head back. He wasn't sure what was happening but every instinct was telling him he needed to go immediately. He had just enough time to put on the harness before the first wave of snow literally fell from the sky, like God opening up a trap door.

In a matter of minutes, CJ was caught in an almost total whiteout. He called out to Cassie, saw a flash of orange coming towards him and managed to clip on her leash, the two of them being blown and battered by the powerful wind. He was grateful that he remembered to put on her vest, if he hadn't she would be completely lost to him out here.

His initial shock turned into survival mode as he grabbed his compass. He watched in disbelief as it shattered in his hand, leaving him lost in the swirling storm, unsure of the way back. He made a decision and trudged ahead with the tree dragging behind and Cassie close at his side. Each step was a chore, the wind was stronger than anything he had ever experienced. The icy sleet constantly assaulted him, like glass shards hitting every exposed inch of his body.

After a while, he felt the terrain change slightly and prayed that his instinct was true, that they would find their way back to the truck, to shelter. CJ was in excellent shape, but the pull and grind of the fierce wind began to wear him down. With a heavy heart, he took off the harness and left the tree behind, knowing his chances were better without it. He hung onto Cassie's leash as they battled the hellish storm together. Inch by inch they went on into the supernatural whiteness, leaving the tree behind to be buried in its wake.

Sourdough

He had never been through anything of the like. The boy and dog were caught up in the worst blizzard Sourdough had ever seen while he watched from under a clear blue mountain sky. He wondered what manner of hoodoo it was that caused this phenomenon, how it was even possible. Not a single snowflake was falling on him while only feet away, the boy was fighting for his life. He continued to track them, watching in awe as the boy and dog painfully navigated their way through the blinding snow, lost in their own separate world.

Sourdough wondered what would happen if he were to run straight at them, if he could break through or somehow switch places with them. Whatever was happening, Sourdough knew that it was not of this world. He mulled over the sickening possibility that he was dead.

He saw the boy drop the tree. He'd figured that would happen, there really was no other choice given the situation. He didn't know why, but Sourdough felt a bit of sadness that he should have gone to so much trouble, only to leave the tree behind. Sourdough knew that the boy was trying to get back to his machine, but had gotten turned around in the storm. He felt a sudden protectiveness, seeing the boy as a kindred spirit. Sourdough figured that if this was it, if he had actually gone under, then he might as well be useful.

Sourdough ran ahead of the boy, still completely untouched by the storm and got out in front of him. He could see that the boy was really tiring, he would need to act quickly if there was to be any chance of survival. His cabin was just a few yards ahead, if the boy could reach it, he would have shelter. That is, if his cabin still existed in whatever world the boy and his dog inhabited.

The dog locked eyes with him through the strange barrier, barking loudly at Sourdough, pulling on the leash and dragging the boy forward. This was it, he thought in sudden joy, this will be his salvation! Sourdough focused all of his energy and let out a whistle that would wake the dead, hootin' and a hollerin' as loud as he could and praying that the dog would follow his lead.

CJ

CJ had never been so tired in all of his life. He tried to focus on every step, willing his feet forward as the relentless wind and cold battered at him. Cassie stayed right by him, every inch the fighter. He would hate to be the cause of her demise. She really had been his very best friend. He wondered if his parents would ever discover where he was, for surely they would find his truck up here someday.

"No! You mustn't give up! Keep moving!"

In his mind he could hear his mother talking to him, see his father's face cheering him on, just like he had at one of his old football games: "Never give up, CJ! Compete! Be your best!"

Again, the bizarre ringing sounds danced around in his head as he continued his futile march against the turbulent storm. He went on for what seemed like a lifetime when he decided that a little rest was just what he needed. If he could stop to close his eyes for just a moment, he would build up the strength to make it back. Just for a minute, no longer.

All of a sudden Cassie went completely crazy, barking and yanking at her leash, almost knocking him over. CJ was instantly jolted awake, scrabbling to stay on his feet and keep up with the dog. She was on a mission. He had never seen her so determined. She pulled him forward at an unrelenting pace, forcing him to follow. He was too exhausted to put up much of a fight, allowing her to take the lead in the hope that she was going in the right direction. On and on they went, dog dragging man until CJ ran headfirst into a hard surface. Snow blind, he put his hands out in front of him and felt the grooved surface of a notched log. He groped around in desperation, putting his frozen hands over every inch until he literally fell through the cabin door.

His first sensation was of Cassie licking his face, both of them miraculously out of the elements. He blinked and slowly looked around at his surroundings. He was in a small cabin. It was warm, the embers of a fire pit were still glowing. He kicked the door shut and fell face down onto a makeshift pallet in one corner. His final thought was of the owner of the cabin and how he would react to finding him here, before sleep finally overtook him. Cassie curled up at his feet, alert and on guard as the merciless storm continued to rage all around them.

Sourdough

Sourdough whooped and hollered as the boy and dog finally made it into the cabin. He couldn't remember the last time he was so relieved about anything. That boy sure had gotten under his skin. He was still dumbstruck that his surroundings were clear and warm while the boy was caught in such a melee. He wasn't sure about the rules of his new situation, but felt an overwhelming urge to go inside and check on his boarder.

The dog was standing at attention, growling as menacingly as possible, which really wasn't much at all. Sourdough entered the room and saw that the boy was dead asleep, the fire just beginning to peter out. He stepped in and held his hand out tentatively to the dog, talking to her in the soothing tones that he always used with Sara whenever she was in a mood.

"Hello, Cassie old girl, I mean you no harm." Sourdough saw the dog relax just a little, but still wary and alert. He reached into his possibles bag and held out a piece of his pemmican jerky, Cassie stepped closer in curiosity.

"I just want to get a look at him, old girl, just for a moment," he said as Cassie reached his hand and gently took the offering. Sourdough patted her on the head, feeling a warmth spread through him that he hadn't felt since his Sara was alive.

He looked the boy over, making sure he was well and covered up. He checked each of his extremities for frostbite and piled him high with his warmest buffalo and deer skin blankets. The boy was lucky. His fingers and toes did not have the telltale signs of black. Sourdough made sure the boy was warm and kept the fire going throughout the night. He washed off his face and refilled the water bin for when the boy awoke the next day. He left out the remainder of his provisions and spent the rest of the night in Cassie's company, petting her soft fur before slipping out into the dawn.

Sourdough quietly made his way back down the hill, the unnatural, shimmering sky lighting his way through the darkness. As he reached the bottom, he could see something in the distance, leaning up against a large aspen tree. The ground around him was still clear as he headed over to the tree to investigate, finding the object partially buried under three feet of fresh snow.

He dropped to his knees and began to dig, his task becoming all the more urgent as he uncovered the frozen body of a man. He could feel his heart pounding out of his chest, or at least what he always thought was a beating heart, as he discovered the identity of the dead man at the base of the tree.

Sourdough let out a slow whistle between his teeth as he gazed upon his own grizzled countenance. Ol' Sourdough had finally gone under, he was well and truly dead, encased in an icy grave upon his own beloved mountain.

CJ

CJ woke up slowly, parts of the dream still playing in his head. *(An old prospector? No. Free man. Mountain man.)* He slowly opened his eyes and saw Cassie laying at his feet. He was piled high with blankets, actually sweating in their warmth. He looked over and saw that there was a bin of water and some sort of food laid out on the table.

"Hello? Is there anyone here?" In response, Cassie came running over, licking him and jumping up in exuberance.

"How did we get here, girl?" he asked, trying hard to remember. "What happened?"

He had vague recollections of fighting through the snow, the terrifying thought of being lost, the sudden horrific storm. The lost tree. He jumped up and threw the cabin door open, expecting the snow to fall in all around him. What he saw actually caused him to gasp in amazement.

The land as far as he can see was bone dry with not a bit of snow in sight, the sun shining down on a perfect winter morning. He stepped out in shock, wondering about his sanity. He looked at the little cabin and walked all around it in complete astonishment. Something caught his eye at the very back of the cabin, a small wooden cross. He walked over to it and saw that it was very old, had been battered and worn throughout many long years.

It simply said "Sara."

CJ and Cassie found their way down the mountain pretty easily. Now that the snow was gone, it didn't take them very long at all. CJ was still trying to decide if he was delusional, combing every inch of the land, looking for any sign of snow as they hiked back to the road. Cassie was her usual, spirited self, leading them down the mountain with gusto. As they turned onto the final bend and his truck came looming into view, CJ felt a sudden jolt of shock. For there, propped up against his old Ford, was the tree. All trussed up and ready to go.

Silent tears ran down his face as he reached the truck, placing his hand upon the trunk of the tree in pure wonder. He said a silent prayer as he loaded it up, Cassie taking her usual spot in the front seat. They drove away with the warm winter sun beaming down and not a single cloud in sight.

Sourdough

Sourdough had to admit that his old cabin had never looked so good. The boy had turned into quite a man over the years, coming up to Santa Fe mountain and making his old shelter into a home. He had kept the original cabin right where it was and built up a great big new one next to it, notching the logs one by one just as Sourdough had done way back when. He had left the old cabin intact, sprucing it up in fine fashion, better than Sourdough could have ever imagined. His family would come here every Christmas, the man taking everyone up to the clearing where he had found his original tree and telling them the story of Sourdough's cabin. Sourdough would stay on the outskirts, feeling like he was part of the family in some small way, proud to bursting of the man the boy had become.

He didn't know why he still lingered on the mountain after all these years, but he didn't mind. His mountain was always a kind of heaven for him, a fitting place for an old mountain man to spend eternity.

Cassie ran over to him, tail wagging. The years had been kind to her, only the snow white of her face marking the passage of time. They turned and walked together over to where two small children were running and playing. The man took the little boy's hand and placed it gently onto the trunk of a pine tree. The girl moved in to join them as the man beamed with pride, carefully handing his daughter the old ax and letting her have the first swing.

Sourdough smiled at the sight of them, happy beyond all measure that they were a part of this land. The inheritors of his mountain. Off in the distance, he could hear the sound of a mule braying. He looked over and saw his Sara waiting for him under the glorious backdrop of a Rocky Mountain winter sky. Finally after all this time, she had come for him.

He said a silent prayer, thanking the Man On High once again for making him a free, mountain man and went to join his old friend. He and Sara set out, ready to take on their new adventure, eager to see what was over the next hill.

Originally published in New Realm in 2017 and Frontier Tales in Issue #98/November 2017

Totality

The entire world had gone mad. Completely bat-shit crazy which was really saying something in this over-sexed, social-media crazed, smartphone obsessed cesspool that made up modern life. Douglas Garuder had long been a man whose time had passed him by. Hell, he still had an ancient flip phone with a long, spidery crack up the screen. Not that he ever used it. Since Joan had passed away some five years ago, there really wasn't anyone he cared to talk to. Most of the time if he even remembered to look at the damn thing, he always expected her to call, reminding him to pick up eggs or some other mundane item at the grocery store. That feeling was always followed by the crushing, black sadness that he would never hear his wife's voice again.

At least not in this life anyway.

He looked down at his watch, another ancient relic that he was always careful to wind and clean. Most of the kids today would get lost trying to read its face with the roman numerals and elegant, thin hands. It was a gift from his old man, the last thing his father ever gave him on the day he left home for good. He had taken Doug's hand in a firm shake, squeezing his son's other arm with as much emotion as he was capable of showing. Doug watched his father through the window for as long as he could, his dad standing in the middle of the dusty road, waving goodbye as the bus carried his only son away to basic training. It would be Doug's last stop before being shipped off to the exotic shores of Vietnam. His father died of a heart attack two weeks later and from that day to this one, he only ever took the watch off to shower.

It was due to happen in just a few minutes. Doug could feel humanity's collective excitement as the eclipse neared its apex. The hype had been going on for weeks, hoards of people clogging the highways along the eclipse's path. It was an event not seen in nearly forty years and not due to come around his part of the world again for another forty. It seemed that just for today, in this hour, that people were putting aside their smartphones and looking up into the heavens much as their ancestors must have done thousands of years before. It was a very humbling thought, a visceral connection to their common past. It felt like a truce, a temporary halt to the endless hostilities and constant infighting of day to day life.

Doug could feel a weight lifting from his soul as the seconds ticked by and the moon began to darken the sun. He could sense Joan here all around him, could picture her as she was on the day that the last total eclipse occurred decades before.

He was the newly-minted principal of Bolingbrook Elementary School and Joan a first-grade teacher. She was vibrant and full of warmth as she helped her little charges put together the cardboard "shadow boxes" they used back then so the kids wouldn't be tempted to look directly at the sun.

Doug was immediately drawn to her, she had an inner beauty that more than matched her outer appearance. Laughing blue eyes and long dark hair that shone in the fading daylight as she took each child outside to view the eclipse's reflection. She didn't react to his bum leg, his limp a souvenir from his last tour in 'Nam. To her, he was a complete man, one she deemed worthy of respect and affection. Doug was a complete goner the moment he looked into her eyes as he introduced himself on that day—they married less than six-months later. She always said that the eclipse had brought them together, it was their heavenly matchmaker.

God how he missed her. It was a constant, physical pain.

A honk from the street below brought Doug out of the memory. From his vantage point ten stories up, he could see the people milling around below like colorful ants. Men and women of every age and creed, stopping in the midst of their busy day to take in the momentous sight. Doug thought they looked like they were going to a 3-D movie, almost every one of them wearing the special glasses that all of the stores were selling out of.

It had been relentlessly hammered into all of their heads that you must never, ever look directly at the eclipse at the risk of your eyesight. He was sick to death of hearing it.

Doug felt a sudden delicate breeze on his face, wondering again if his wife was present. The eclipse was almost complete, he could feel the darkness taking over the light. It was disorienting that night should conquer the day at eleven-thirty in the morning, Doug was not surprised that strange things seemed to happen during these events. It was a primordial, palpable feeling. He could almost hear the collective intake of breath from the people below as time seemed to stop. Totality had finally been achieved.

Doug took a deep breath of fresh air and carefully removed his watch, lovingly setting it onto the ledge. It was his one real regret in life that he and Joan were never able to have children, he had no one to pass his only keepsake on to. He hoped that someone would take it in, it really was a good watch. They didn't make them like that anymore, quality had been sacrificed on the altar of instant gratification. He wouldn't miss that, not even one little bit.

He stretched up to his full height on the ledge, propping himself up with his ever-present cane and finally turned his face up to the sky to meet his heavenly matchmaker.

Oh my God, Joanie, it's beautiful, magnificent!

Doug could see the edges of light attempting to escape around the moon, glorious in its rich blackness. Besides his wife's face, it was the most beautiful thing he had ever seen and he stared at it for as long as he could keep his eyes open. He could hear her then, calling his name, her voice was like music to his battered old ears and Doug knew that the time had come.

He could still see the eclipse, it was etched onto his eyes as he turned away from it and got himself ready. He had lived a good life, a good as he was able but really, he had only been going through the motions for five long years.

Douglas Garuder discarded his cane, shedding it like an old skin. He would not miss it, not even one little bit. He lifted his arms high above his head and leapt from the ledge in a semi-graceful swan dive, plunging headfirst down to the concrete below and into his wife's waiting arms.

Totality had finally been achieved.

Originally published in "Literally Stories," August 2017

Terrible Beauty

The woman ran as fast as she was able through the thick brush, the noose around her neck trailing behind with every step. Her feet were bloody and bruised, her face brutalized beyond recognition. The lake was almost in sight. All she had to do was get there. She had always been a good swimmer and the years on the trail had served her well. If she could just get to the water, she might have a chance.

The man that hired her offered a great deal of money, enough to get by on for a long time. Foolishly, she believed him. A "soiled dove" had to be on guard out on the frontier, and up to now, she'd always been a good judge of character.

He threw her into a wagon behind the brothel, ferreting her away before anyone was the wiser. He brought her to a group of ragged men standing around an enormous fire, the flames illuminating the open prairie like stolen daylight. She knew then they were going to sacrifice her once they had their fill. She was to be some sort of carnal offering which if truth be told, was the only logical end to a life filled with so much pain. She clawed and kicked as they struggled to hoist her up, her considerable form weighing down the branch. The evil men chanted and sang, throwing cups of rotgut whiskey onto the bonfire. When the old rope snapped, she raced into the night.

The animal instinct for survival was fueling her escape. Well, that and the promise of the lake, the waters washing away her many sins. The lake was small, but offered a cool respite. An end to her troubles at long last.

If she could only make it to the water.

A shot rang out behind her, the blood pounding in her ears as she finally reached the lake's edge. She dove, fingers reaching out for the water when the second shot rang out. It took off the top of her skull as she crested into a final dive, her death throes cleansed in the icy cold water.

A true sacrifice had been made in blood and rage and exquisite fear. As time and the elements dried up the lake and bleached her shattered old bones, she slept. She slept over all the long years until they tamed the land, paving over her. Their city was erected atop her unmarked grave and still she slept. That changed when the water called her back through the mists of time. Always, she'd been drawn to the water. She was no longer anything remotely human, except in appearance. Ruled by hunger, insatiable and horrible, it gnawed constantly at her tormented soul. She knew it was time to feed.

She was a goddess, some sort of water nymph. He couldn't explain how he knew this or even exactly what that meant, but he was convinced it was so. Rising up on a cloud of warm mist, shimmering and wet, every part of her called out to him as he felt the first familiar stirrings of arousal. He watched her hungrily as she came towards him, water dripping from her spiked fingernails, naked and unashamed. All curves and rounded mounds of flesh, like a statue of some ancient fertility goddess he had seen once in a cheesy B-movie. Large hips with fully packed haunches, her bulbous breasts swung softly from side to side as she walked, slowly and deliberately through the steam.

Aldo Costa liked his women on the larger side, always had, which was amusing to many of his peers considering his own condensed stature. He couldn't contain his growing excitement as a seductive smile danced across her lips, his left eye twitching involuntarily. Her face was heartbreakingly beautiful in its perfection. Large, enchanting, sea-foam green eyes beamed at him, her long purple-black hair hanging in thick waves well past her ponderous hips. He could envision playfully pulling her head back, a fistful of hair in each hand as she screamed in unbridled ecstasy above him. Closer and closer she came, water splashing at her feet with every step as she flickered in and out of his sight.

She was a mirage, billowing steam, and magic as she reached out to him and roughly yanked his towel away. A single claw-like nail gently caressed the side of his face before digging deeper, causing a drop of blood to dance down his cheek as she simultaneously gripped his manhood with her other hand. Costa sucked in his breath and she smiled, revealing a mouthful of razor-sharp, jagged teeth. Multiple rows of predatory teeth gleamed in the mist, menacing and shark-like as her mouth grew impossibly large in a blood-curdling rictus of a smile. Costa watched ropes of drool falling to the ground from her serrated fangs as she laughed, a sound like a throat full of broken glass. He could feel his pulse hammering through his neck, an offering for the beast as she moved in closer for their first, deadly embrace.

★

Costa woke up in terror, falling to the tile and unceremoniously smacking the side of his head on the slippery steam room floor. He must have dozed off for a moment, a very dangerous thing to do in here. Thankfully, he was still alone. The steam billowed out in regular intervals, enveloping him. It was not a big room at all. Costa found the local hole-in-the-wall gym to be much more intimate than the larger chains in town. It was the perfect place to conduct any business that needed to be done. It was a win-win situation all around in normal times, but this time was anything but normal.

He swore he had seen the dream-woman before, wished very much to see her again, despite her awful smile. The old farts at Paul's Gym swore the place was haunted by a stacked broad with sharp talons for nails, walking around in the nude. Like any of those birds would have the slightest idea about what to do with such a delicious creature, but Costa knew. Oh man, did he know. Aldo didn't believe in spooks, at least not up until today, but he figured if he had to be haunted by something, she would certainly do. More likely, he was cracking up under the pressure of his latest situation.

Aldo was well aware he had far greater things to fear than ghosts. Real life monsters were closing in on him which is why he was at Paul's, late on a Sunday night when he should have been halfway across the state of Illinois by now, Chicago firmly in his rear view mirror. The prick who hired him to do the job on West Schiller Street owed him his cut. What the bastard neglected to mention was the house belonged to a favorite cousin of the biggest family boss in the city. Costa figured he'd better collect his money and skedaddle, there was no sense in waiting around to be fitted with concrete shoes.

The guy was supposed to meet him well over an hour ago. Costa's entire life was packed up in the car and ready to go. He had just enough saved up to get him by, but he really need that goddamned money. It was going to give him a fresh start or at least a head start. Aldo knew the man was going to be a no-show and he'd have to come back to collect another time. He would enjoy putting a cap in the asshole's head for his trouble, but it would have to wait. He hated the thought of leaving without the money, but he hated the thought of being dead even worse.

As much as he didn't want to admit it, it was definitely time for Aldo Costa to hit the road.

Costa bent over and picked up the discarded towel off of the floor, his erection still painful from his arousing dream. He toweled himself off a bit, taking a brief moment, as he always did, to admire his chiseled state. Wherever he ended up, he would definitely need to find a place like this, it pained him to have to leave it.

A new blast of steam rose up around him. He had been in here longer than usual and felt the effects of the sweat and dehydration as he picked up his water bottle, taking a long swig.

He always tipped Paul on his way out, throwing a twenty his way for an extra few minutes in the steam room before the man closed up for the night. Costa made sure to take care of people, knew the power of tipping and collecting favors. It had served him well, at least to this point in his life.

Through the foggy glass he could tell the gym was empty. Paul would be looking to lock up and collect his nightly due. Costa sighed. He knew Paul would be anxious to get home to his wife and newborn son. Costa always took the time to get to know those who were in his purview. You never knew when a personal touch could lead to an advantage. Tonight, he would tip the man an extra fifty in gratitude. Costa was feeling a bit nostalgic and could afford to be generous one last time.

He figured he could put in at least twelve hours and two states of driving before having to rest. If he left now, he could take a quick shower on the way out. The man was not coming. He had better make his peace with that and live to fight another day.

As he made his way to the glass doors, the first prick of unease tickled the back of his neck. Costa always had an acute sense of danger which had gotten him out of more than a few scrapes over the years. The lights in the main gym turned off all at once.

The water beaded on the glass. He used a corner of the towel to wipe it away as a fresh batch of steam blasted him. Costa squinted through the watery pane, trying to make out the shapes in the room beyond. Another light went out in the pool room directly outside the spa as he noticed a large shape lying prone on the floor. He instinctively ducked down and reached behind him for his weapon, realizing that his pistol was safely stowed away in locker 21B of the men's changing room down the hall. He'd lost his edge, there was no doubt about it.

His eyes slowly adjusted to the new change in light and he could see the shape in question was Paul. Blood was pooled around his bashed-in skull dripping into the pool, turning the over-chlorinated water a bright, angry red. He identified small chunks of Paul's brain matter floating in the gory water. It looked like the manager would not be making it home to his pretty young wife after all. Costa's careless arrogance had cost the man his life, depriving an infant of his father. He knew then this was to be personal, vengeance of the first order. Old school: family-style retribution. He would be very, very lucky to make it out of here alive.

"Fuck!" He spat through clenched teeth as another light went out in the main office, leaving him almost completely in the dark. The only lights left were the muted ones in the steam room. Costa had no interest in getting murdered in a dark sauna. He decided to take his chances in the gym, despite being naked and unarmed. Concealing his body behind the first bench, he slowly reached up to the door handles.

Coiled like a spring, he yanked hard, nearly banging his face on the door. The door wouldn't budge. In a blind panic, he tried both door handles again, shaking them violently over and over as he realized the true horror of his predicament. He saw a rusty crowbar had been jammed through the outer handles of the steam room doors, trapping him inside. The remaining lights went out and he was plunged into complete blackness. The hiss of newly-made steam was his only company in the dark.

Costa hunkered down on the floor away from the glass, willing himself to slow his shallow breathing and remain calm. Aside from the hissing steam, there was not a single sound to be heard. Costa tried to focus, searching desperately for any trace of noise or activity. He waited for what seemed like a lifetime, before tentatively standing up and attempting to peer through the glass door.

The darkness seemed to be alive, gathering and dissipating like the steam itself. As his eyes slowly became accustomed to his new reality, a small green light in the corner of the spa drew his attention. He carefully made his way over to it, its unearthly glow illuminating a large enough patch in the pitch-black steam room for him to be able to see his watch.

Thank God I spent the extra coin for the waterproof feature, Costa thought in amusement as he found the button and the watch face lit up like a beacon in a storm. He had been in here for over twenty minutes, already getting to the top end of his usual time. Usually, around thirty minutes was the most he could handle before heading to the shower.

Keep it together Aldie, you're gonna need all of your shit-for-brains to get out of this clusterfuck!

Costa moved backwards and banged his leg hard on the wooden bench. He turned around in the dark holding the glowing watch face out like a shield in front of him, searching frantically through the misty darkness for the source of the voice.

"Shit, Squirrel, is that you? What the hell are you doing in here?" He spat out in pure fear, the voice of his childhood friend and one-time cellmate making the hairs rise on the back of his neck.

Oh, you know I'm always around Aldo-Nova. You'll never shake me. Ain't gonna happen.

From somewhere outside the gym, Costa heard a car door slam followed by wheels squealing out of the parking lot. Not very subtle, but then subtlety was never the boss' strong suit. At least now, without the henchmen lurking around, he was able to recognize his greatest threat. The steam room was one A-class, fuck-all of a problem, but Costa was now afraid of something much worse—the total loss of his mind. The vision of the water woman was disturbing enough without adding more fuel to the fire.

There was no way Squirrel could be talking to him. His best friend had been killed in a brutal prison fight over four years ago, had bled out in Costa's arms right there on the concrete floor of their dingy old cell.

Costa sat down heavily on the wooden bench, holding his head in his hands. He reached down and took a sip of his water bottle, trying to formulate some kind of plan to get out of this mess—something that didn't require talking to ghosts.

Aldie, don't be an asshole, OK? You need to ration your water until we can figure a way out of this, Squirrel's nasally voice was relentless.

Aldo clenched his eyes shut and put his hands over his ears like a small child, trying to tune out the voice of his dead friend.

"Cut it out, Squirrel! I am not hearing you, this is not happening!"

Look buddy, I don't have to tell you that you are in a world of hurt here. I may be dead, but I'm not a stubborn jackass! I'm here to help, you moron....

Costa stood up in a blind panic and ran full tilt at the glass doors, slipping on the wet floor before reaching them and banging his head hard on the left-side door. The reverberation of the reinforced glass pane rang out in the small room, causing his ears to ring violently as he went down hard, losing consciousness. The last thing he heard was his friend's voice frantically calling out to him in the darkness.

She was made to be worshiped—created for tribute, bloodsport and unending sacrifice. Costa saw her again as she ascended from the vapor, the steam and mist whipping her long hair about her shoulders. An old, ratty noose hung around her neck and he could see the angry grooves in the flesh of her neck where she had been lynched. What had been her crime, he wondered weakly, that she should have been hung for it? It seemed such an immense waste.

He got the immediate impression she lived and thrived in the water, the swirling mists she called home obeying her every whim. He laid flat on his back on the steam room floor, looking up in fascination at the vision of her as she made her way back over to him through the spray and shadows. Costa could make out tuneless chanting in the background, the smell of fire and fear and sulfur filling up his lungs to bursting.

God! How had he ever lived this long without her? How he adored her! He wanted to get lost in her luminous pale-green eyes as she mounted him, pinning his wrists down above his head and reaching down to nuzzle his neck. She unhinged her immense jaw of knife-edged teeth, her rancid breath hot and salty on his throat as he squirmed with pleasure, giving himself up to her completely and utterly. She flickered in and out like an old-time movie, her face morphing from perfect to mutilated and back again. One eye hung loosely from its socket, the other was completely sealed shut. He reached up to touch her battered face as she lowered herself to the soft part of his neck, ready for her feast at long last. If this was the price he must pay to possess her, he would do it gladly, willingly. They would live in the mist forever as master and slave. No one would ever hurt her again...

GODDAMMIT, ALDO! WAKE UP! WAKE UP, FOR CHRIST'S SAKE!

The creature hissed, angrily dissipating back into the steam as Costa shot up from the floor in pain and confusion. Squirrel's voice filled his throbbing head, ricocheting off of the steam room walls, coming at him from every direction all at once in an earsplitting volume.

"Christ, Squirrel! You always were a pain in the ass!" he yelled out to the darkness, "God, my head, it's on fire!"

I'm telling you, Aldie, that bitch is bad news! If you give in to her, it's lights out, game over for good, capisce? She will eat your soul. Trust me on this, you need to stay awake.

Costa shook his head and held his all-important watch out to the dark, searching for any sign of the woman, ghost or whatever it was that had him so enthralled. Wherever she was, it was not with him now. He felt a sharp pang of longing, sorrow that she had gone.

I don't think you're hearing me, bro. If you get with her, you are dead. Period. We need to focus on keeping you awake, it's only in dreams that she can hurt you. We can find a way out of this. We've done it before.

The timer for the ever-present steam machine let off another healthy blast. Costa figured that he had now been in here for well over an hour. He could feel the weakness in his bones, sapping him of all of his vaunted strength. It occurred to him that since he had already lost his mind, that he might as well travel all the way down the road to Crazyville with his deceased friend and a voluptuous steam-demon.

"Yeah, but we didn't find a way out of that last one, did we Squirrel?" His voice sounded very small as an overwhelming sadness came over him. Tears sprang to his eyes, a sensation that Costa hadn't felt since that awful day.

"Why'd you get in the way, Squirrel? I could have handled it! You didn't have to take the fall. You never did." Costa saw him again in his mind. Squirrel bleeding out on the floor, his throat cut by a homemade shank that was supposed to be coming for Costa. Costa sobbed like a small child, desperately trying to hold his friend's blood in his body until help arrived.

As always, Squirrel stood in the way—his only true friend in the world. God, how he missed him.

You know why, Aldo. You're better than all of this shit, that's why. You were the only person who was ever decent to me. Now you gotta be decent to yourself. Stay awake, Aldo and think!

Costa sat back on the bench and wet his lips with the water bottle, following Squirrel's advice to conserve. His senses were fading and he knew it would only be a matter of time before he would want to close his eyes again—for more reasons than one. Damn her!

The gym was run down, that was what attracted Costa to it in the first place. Maybe there would be something he could use in the room to try to escape. He groped around the old wooden bench and found that one of the boards was beginning to come loose. Costa grabbed onto it like a lifeline. He went to work trying to pry it off as Squirrel chattered away inanely in the background, keeping him sufficiently annoyed to stay awake, at least for the time being.

'*We built this city. We built this city on rock and roll! Built this city, we built this city on rock...*'

"All right, Squirrel, could you at least try to sing it in tune, for fuck's sake?" Costa said in frustration as his friend belted out the old '80s tune over and over. Squirrel had a thing for classic rock, apparently still did, even from the Great Beyond.

Don't be a hater, Aldo-Wan-Kenobi. The Force, strong in you is not.

Costa had now spent nearly two hours in the sweltering steam room and had somehow managed to pry off most of a full-length, half-rotted wooden board from the bench, wrenching it free in one final burst of strength before falling back against the wall.

"I'm done, my friend. I need a little break, just for a moment" he said, closing his bloodshot eyes. His water bottle had only about two sips left in it if he was lucky, he was quickly becoming lethally dehydrated in here. He wondered in morbid fascination what they would discover when they found his body. Would he be boiled alive in his own brain-juices? Cooked like a side of pulled pork at a barbecue? He began to laugh hysterically at the possibilities before letting himself slowly begin to drift off.

Hey, dumbass! Stop being such a wuss, stand up for a minute d'ya hear me? Get up, Costa! ALDO!

Costa felt a warm, tingling sensation as she began to gather in the corner. If he could just get Squirrel to finally shut up and give them some privacy.

ALDOALDOALDOALDO!

Not this time, old pal, he said in his mind as she assembled herself in all of her imperious glory, right there in front of him. He had never seen anything so beautiful, so superb with beads of water gathering on her naked skin as she shimmered in the shining mist. She smiled her familiar, macabre grin in triumph, preparing to take him, as was her due.

Costa heard her voice for the first time, an ethereal humming. Her voice was breathy and light. The strange chanting started up again all around them, an angry cacophony, whooping and drunken laughter. Above the crescendo of noise was Squirrel, screaming at him to wake up. The watery ghost reached out to him, her hand covered in dried bits of gore. The top of her scalp flapped over to one side as she leaned in to embrace him once and for all. He leaned out to her, entranced, ready to join with her in the water for all eternity.

Just then a door slammed in the outer gym, waking Costa out of his reverie as Squirrel whooped and hollered all around him. Her vision disintegrated and returned to the steam in an angry whoosh, hissing and malevolent. Costa felt jolts of adrenaline surging through him at the possibility of someone being out there to help him. He flattened himself up against the far wall and waited, wanting to assess the level of threat before yelling for help.

Easy Aldo, let's just wait and see. Be ready for anything.

A shadow crept along the perimeter of the outside room, making its way around to Paul's body before unceremoniously kicking it into the pool in a splash of gore. Costa's eyes were so adjusted to the dark he could easily make out the man's build and height, instinctively knew he was up to no good. Squirrel whispered in his ear, low and conspiratorial.

They came back, Aldo. They mean to finish you. Get ready Aldie, we may only get one shot at this.

Costa stayed back in the shadows, terrified that the man would turn the lights on and expose him. He could see the man press his face up to the glass door and peer in, searching for him, using the sleeve of his fancy suit to wipe the condensation away for a better view. Not finding his prey, the figure raised his weapon and began to slowly pull the crowbar out of the door handles.

"I can't do it, Squirrel. I'm too weak," he whispered into the room, feeling like he would pass out at any moment. He had never been more exhausted, or more defeated. He began to feel her in the room again, gaining strength.

Bullshit, Costa! Be a man for once in your miserable, back-asswards life and pick it up. Be a man, you bastard! PICK. IT. UP. NOW!

A great blast of cold air entered the room as the man cautiously stepped inside with gun raised. Costa took his first real breath of fresh air in almost three hours, giving him one final burst of energy as he brought the old wooden board crashing down on the man's hand. The gun flew off into the shadows as the man jumped up in surprise. Costa summoned every ounce of strength and hit the man in the face, nail side up, with his makeshift weapon. His attacker went down as Costa rode the final waves of his strength, punching the man repeatedly before falling backwards, completely spent.

He could hear Squirrel screaming at him to get up and get out, there might be more coming. Costa could also hear her desperately calling out to him, begging him to stay with her. Her voice became low and seductive, rich and full of promise, everything he could have ever dreamed of in a woman. She was powerful, irresistible. Costa began to feel the old excitement building in his loins until Squirrel cut in, singing offkey, at full volume in his right ear. He always was a huge mood kill.

WE BUILT THIS CITY! WE BUILT THIS CITY ON ROCK AND ROLL, BUILT THIS...

Without any further prompting, Aldo Costa pulled the unconscious man into the steam room and sat him up on the bench. He could hear the man start to moan lightly as the mist began to collect for her return. It was well past time for Aldo to hit the road. The man's suit was Armani, a fine cut, not too far off from his own size. Costa figured it might just do in a pinch. Before relieving him of his gun, Costa took a final look around what was supposed to be his watery tomb. Squirrel had suddenly gone silent, his buddy standing in the way of him and disaster one final time. This time, he was determined not to let Squirrel's sacrifice go to waste.

As he closed the steam room doors, Costa decided that his new life would start right at that moment. He threw the crowbar to the ground, taking a moment to pull Paul's body out of the water and cover his face with a towel. If the evil bastard inside the steam room could escape the Terrible Beauty, more power to him, but Costa wouldn't kill him. As much as he wanted his revenge, he decided to run. He stopped only long enough to put up the "closed" sign in the front window and make sure the door was locked behind him. Aldo Costa was finally going legit.

She watched him through the watery pane as he ran away, abandoning her to the hunger. It was agonizing, all encompassing. Her tormentors started up their hellish incantations once more, torturing her from the very depths of hell. Feeding would be the only way to hold them at bay until she could gain strength. Limb from limb, she would devour them all.

The man on the bench began to come to. This one was so much more delicious, more evil than the last, he would make an exquisite sacrifice. She raised her arm and the crowbar began to rattle and climb up the glass wall until it took its rightful place in the door handles, locking them back in. There was no guardian spirit in here with this one, she could afford to take her time.

As the man opened his eyes, she smiled slowly, licking her lips with excitement. Each step was deliberate and tantalizing as she made her way over to him, swaying her hips seductively. The rope of the noose hung down her back like a coronation robe. After she fed on this one, there would be another and another after that. Her hunger would not be assuaged until she had taken her revenge. One man was as good as the next, it made no difference. They had never brought her anything but devastation.

He was fully awake now, holding his arms out to her as she moved in for the kill. Her gruesome smile would be his final vision as he bucked and screamed under her in a mixture of pleasure and pain. The mist and water circled around them in their coupling, feeding the beast in a blood-soaked orgy of sacrifice. The Terrible Beauty was meant to be worshiped, had discovered her true calling. She had, at long last, found a home.

The man in the fine Armani suit stood at the grave site, talking in a low voice and wiping away tears. At the very end of his visit, he reverently placed a well-worn sports watch on top of the headstone, gently touching the engraving of his friend's name before turning away. He got into his car and sped away, opening it up to full speed on the highway, windows down and an old Jefferson Starship song blaring.

He decided to go west, somewhere landlocked, with minimal rain and water. It was as good a plan as any, a new life just over the horizon. Aldo Costa was finally free.

The body was unrecognizable. The skin, where any remained, had sloughed off the corpse in big, greasy chunks. It was a grotesque spectacle, making even the most seasoned detective throw up. The biggest mystery was what manner of monster had completely ripped the throat out of the man. The body was seated, dismembered except for one leg and a torso that still sat on the bench of the sauna. His head was attached, but just barely. It had lopped over to one side, a few stray tendons stubbornly holding it in place. A piece of his windpipe sat in a bloody puddle on the sauna floor like someone had spat it out in disgust.

The door to the main gym had been locked with the "closed" sign up so no one had been in here for over ten days, the regular customers assuming Paul had taken a well-deserved vacation. The steam room was on, all of that time, at the very highest temperature it would go with a rusty crowbar inserted through the door handles. Out by the pool, the body of the owner laid with his skull bashed in, blackened with rot and desiccation. It was a scene from a nightmare.

In the end, they decided the John Doe in the sauna must be one Aldo Costa, who had done time for grand larceny and a dozen other lesser crimes. He was the last one who had checked into the rec center that night, so it only made sense that it would be him. There were no fingerprints as his fingers had liquefied. DNA was a real possibility if they could get an uncorrupted sample in that soupy mess. They didn't know who had killed him so viciously, but the odds were it was related to his unfortunate line of work. Maybe Costa even killed the night manager himself before meeting his just desserts with the crime family? It would be one hell of an ongoing investigation. The detective knew if the press ever got wind of the gruesome details, it would be a shitstorm. So for now, they were trying to lay low.

The detective thought the world was well rid of a hustler like Costa. It would save the taxpayers' money in having to incarcerate him in the future. No, a low-life thief like Aldo Costa would not be missed.

The only thing the detective could not stop thinking about was the look on what was left of Costa's grotesque face. It had given him nightmares for weeks afterward. The corpse had an enormous, leering grin, like he was the happiest bastard ever to walk the earth. The detective could not for the life of him understand what pleasure could be found in such a gruesome death. It gave him the chills.

Eventually, it became a source of obsession for the man, seeing that mangled face in his dreams until he began to vividly fantasize about water, inexplicably drawn to a beautiful, curvy figure rising up from the mist. He decided that he needed to go back to Paul's Gym and get the lay of the land, maybe even try out the sauna.

After that, the detective finally understood. He understood all too well, but by then, he really didn't care.

Originally published in "Pilcrow&Dagger," February/March 2018 issue

The Park

The old man went to the park every day, sitting on the third bench from the left. He planted himself on the right side each time, his cane perched alongside and a half-bag of birdseed resting in his lap.

He was withered and stooped, shuffling along to his spot. The birds followed behind him in a pack, screeching in their hunger. No one knew his age. The deep wrinkles carved into his grizzled old face could have pegged him from seventy to one-hundred, or anywhere in between.

He was a fixture at the park, part of the scenery like the pair of ancient fir trees that had been guarding the perimeter for decades. He'd been there so long that no one thought to ask what his life was like, where he was from. He was just the old man at the park, he simply was. Like those old trees, or the hill, or the run-down playground that kids from every era had run and frolicked and skinned their knees upon.

Generations of them passing by, growing up while the old man fed his birds in solitude.

He'd seen the little girl at the park for the past few weeks, running the wrong way up the slide in her frilly pink dress.

She looked to be around five or six, but the man's eyesight was failing, he couldn't be sure of anything except for his pigeons.

He had names for many of them, knew them on sight. One fat pigeon had a black ring around his left eye and was bolder than the rest, venturing up onto the bench and sidling right up to his leg, even allowing the old man to lightly touch the feathers on top of his head. The old man called him "Buddy" and was content to spend the afternoons with the bird perched next to him and an entire flock of Buddy's cooing brethren milling at his feet.

The children and their watchful mothers weren't quite sure what to think of the old man, mostly giving him and his flock a wide berth, but not the little girl. She ran boldly up to the bench, the red ball she was chasing completely forgotten as she stared intently at him.

"It was a dog, you know," she said to him in a clear, decisive tone. "Buddy. He wasn't a bird, he was a Rough Collie."

The old man sat in open-mouthed astonishment as the little girl ran away, heeding the call of her nervous mother, for little girls must never, ever talk to strangers.

He thought back to his youth, many, many years ago and remembered the sable Lassie dog that his mother had brought home on his seventh birthday. The dog was multi-colored with thick, long hair. The most beautiful creature he had ever laid eyes on, his very best friend.

He'd forgotten after so many years that he named the dog Buddy and that the dog had a very unique characteristic. Buddy had one black ring encircling his left eye.

The old man looked for the peculiar little girl over the next few days, disappointed by her absence and anxious to see her again. How had she known about his childhood pet? Indeed, how had she known before he'd even remembered it?

Buddy, of course! That's who the bird reminded me of, it was so obvious.

The red ball went flying through the old man's flock, birds angrily lifting off into the sky as the little girl came running into view. She circled the bench twice, the old man craning his stiff neck to watch her. She stopped and climbed up onto the bench, her little legs hanging over the side as the old man regarded her cautiously.

"You always did love animals, Bobby. So much more so than your brother Jack, do you remember?"

The old man looked into her innocent young face, wondering how on earth this little child could possibly know his childhood name and that of his brother, who had died over twenty years before. He cleared his throat to speak and found a lump rising there, rendering him speechless. She took his gnarled, old hand into her own tiny one.

"It's alright Bobby. You were always the sensitive child, my sweet baby."

He heard a voice in the distance, urgently calling out, the little girl's mother getting worried as she hopped down off of the bench and went to retrieve her ball.

"Wait!" he said in a rush, "is this possible? Is it you?"

The little girl gave him a big, lopsided smile revealing two missing front teeth. A sudden memory tugged at his heart, his mother bending over him brightly smiling, handing him a large red ball. She wore a floral print dress, her long hair plaited high atop her head as they played in the park on a brilliant summer day. She had been gone for so many years now, how could he have forgotten?

"Goodbye my boy, I know we will meet again," she said in parting as she ran back to the park and into her mother's arms, leaving the old man behind in complete wonderment.

After that, the old man could always be found at the park playing with the children, always searching for her. He was remarkably spry for his advanced age, allowing the children to feed his large flock of birds including one incredibly tame pigeon named Buddy.

He became a sought-out companion, the children and birds all flocking around him in mutual admiration.

They found the old man there on his bench one glorious autumn afternoon, surrounded by his birds and a tiny five-year-old girl. She was there holding his hand as he took his final breath, in the same park where he had played with his mother so many years ago.

She lovingly closed his eyes before running back to the park carrying a large red ball.

Originally published in "Quail Bell Review," March 2017

The Earworm

Black Jack didn't mean to kill the old man. It really was an accident of time and place—the old man actually coming home at the same time that Jack was robbing the place. Completely not his fault! The old bastard should have kept to his daily schedule. If he had, he would still be above ground doing old people shit and Black Jack would be in Vegas, tight as a drum and rolling dice, with a high-end hooker perched on each knee. Jack had spent weeks following him, with each day as skull-crushingly boring as the next.

The man would leave the house every morning at exactly 7:15, get into his beat-up old black Lincoln and putter down the highway at a speedy 44 miles an hour, causing Jack and the rest of humanity to scream and honk at him the entire way. Not that old gramps could hear them—he was practically deaf, after all.

Hell, maybe Jack had done the world a favor—at least the drivers of the world that is— someone oughta give him a freaking medal.

The old man would pull into the cemetery by 8:10 and spend the next hour doing God knows what at the small, white headstone at the top of the hill, while Black Jack contemplated jumping off of a bridge to cure his boredom.

Then the long, tortured drive home, by way of the local gas station, where old Pops would get one small coffee and a newspaper—like anyone other than ancient old goats still read newspapers anymore. Jack knew for a fact that the man didn't even own a computer or a cell phone—that's how clueless he was.

The rest of the day was filled with napping, shuffling around the yard with a garden hose and reading. On a really exciting day, the old man might actually take a walk down to the mailbox, only to spend an eternity opening and reading through every stinking thing, even the junk mail.

Dinner was at 5:30 sharp, followed by his evening constitutional in the can. Then he would watch old, boring sitcoms on a tiny old TV. Everything was old, old, old. He would usually fall asleep on the couch around 7:45, then drag his tired old ass to bed by 8:30. The next day would be the same. Wash, rinse, repeat then start all over again.

Every. Fucking. Day.

The only reason Jack even gave a shit about any of this was because his one-time cellmate Ed knew a guy who knew a guy who said that the old fart was loaded, had a fortune stashed away in the walls somewhere.

Gold Krugerrands (whatever the hell those were) jewelry, cash, you name it, and all of it walled up in the man's crappy, old rundown house. Black Jack knew that the man's wife had died some years back and that his kids didn't come around much. In other words, he was the perfect mark.

Jack planned it all out perfectly, down to the minute, knowing that he had almost two full hours before the old man would come shambling in with his cup of cold coffee. Breaking in was no great shakes, Black Jack knew his way around a lock alright.

He let himself in, crowbar in hand, tearing through each tiny room, leaving no stone unturned. The walls were thin and crumbled easily, allowing Jack to get through each room in record time. He had blasted through the entire first floor when he heard a faint sound, music, wafting up from the old man's basement. Jack instantly froze, his every nerve on fire. He knew that the old man hardly ever went in the basement, probably because he was too feeble to make it up and down the stairs anymore. There was no reason in the world why anyone should be down there, but Jack heard it all the same.

"From the halls of Montezuma, to the shores of Tripoli..."

Black Jack flattened himself against the wall, completely silent and listened again..."*We will fight our country's battles on the land and on the sea..."*

Black Jack crept down the stairs, stealthy as any cat burglar and burst into the room, crowbar held out in front of him like a sword. There was no one there, it was completely empty—just a partially finished room with a huge picture wall.

He pulled the string to the lone light bulb and was instantly barraged by images of the old man, from every stage of his life, covering the entire wall. Pictures of him in uniform, in camouflage, with a beautiful young woman and children. Medals in cases were set among the pictures in a disorganized cluster, one Jack noted, was in a frame labeled "Purple Heart."

Damn, Jack thought, this guy was hardcore.

There were pictures and documents everywhere, awards, citations and an enormous, red flag of the US Marine Corps.

The singing suddenly started up again, a little louder now, some sort of deranged choir and Jack nearly jumped out of his skin frantically searching for the source.

"First to fight for right and freedom...."

He turned in every direction, holding the crowbar out, ready for the attack, but still there was nothing. No radio, no TV, just him alone in the creepy room. I must be losing it, he thought, I'd better find the loot and get the hell out of here.

Jack began to smash up the wall, shards of glass and old pictures flying in every direction. A piece of glass shot out and hit him right in the cheek, inflaming him even further. Blood streaking down his face, he continued his carnage, all the frustration and endless doldrums of the past few weeks coming out in a great, violent spasm. The last thing to hit the ground was the case with the Purple Heart and Jack felt a slight twinge of conscience (a real first for him), knowing what the old man must have gone through to get it.

He suddenly noticed that the music had stopped, it was as quiet as a tomb in there. Out of breath and feeling more than a little out of shape, Black Jack set the crowbar aside and bent down to pick up the medal. He had just grabbed it when he heard the tell-tale click directly behind him and knew, in a moment of dread, that he was definitely not alone.

"Drop it asshole," the old man said in a deadly calm voice that sounded a hell of a lot younger than Jack knew he actually was.

Jack instinctively raised his arms up into the air, the Purple Heart dangling out of one hand like a child's toy, swinging back and forth in slow motion. He only had a split second to process that the gun was leveled right at him before he threw the medal in the man's face and charged him head on.

A huge, explosive boom filled the air. The old man, shocked by Jack's sudden attack, had shot into the wall where Jack had just been standing. Jack tackled him at full speed, both of them going down in a violent struggle. The old man kneed him right in the nuts and stuck his thumb directly into Jack's left eye causing him to bellow with rage and pain, blood spurting out in a great red arc.

The gun had flown out of the man's grip in all the chaos, hitting the floor right behind Jack in a metallic thunk. Jack snapped his head back and head butted the man full on, causing him to fall over backwards as Jack frantically scrambled for the pistol. He barely managed to get it in his grip before the old man sucker-punched him in the gut, Jack doubling over and reaching out for the man's legs to bring him down.

Falling in a heap once again, they both grabbed for the gun, pulling and struggling with inhuman effort. This old bastard is one mean son of a bitch, Jack thought in a panic as he finally got his grip around the handle and pulled the trigger.

BOOM!

Black Jack wasn't sure at first which of the two of them took the hit. He was dizzy with pain and fear, half blind, with an awful buzzing and ringing in his ears from the gunshot.

The old man was laying on top of him, a dead weight. Jack pushed him off like a limp rag doll, then scrabbled away, his breath wheezing and labored. The old man's eyes stared vacantly up at him, a look of defiance still etched onto his dead face as if to give Jack one final "fuck you" from the Great Beyond.

"I've got to hand it to you, you old son of a bitch, you went out like a champ." Jack said out loud to the dead man, "Who knew you had it in you?"

Jack saw the Purple Heart bunched up on the floor, scooped it up and put it into his pocket as a token that he had won this fight. Granted, he'd gotten his ass pretty well kicked by an eighty-year-old man, but he would take the credit all the same.

"And to keep our honor clean! We are proud to claim the title of United States Marines!"

Jack snapped back hard into the destroyed wall, stars clouding his vision. He caught his foot on a picture frame and went down like a ton of bricks, landing on top of the old man one last time before leaping to his feet and running back up the stairs with the music following from behind.

He ran out of there like his ass was on fire, screaming in terror as the supernatural music tracked him the entire way. Jack didn't have another coherent thought until he was roaring down the highway, pedal to the floor. He was halfway home before he noticed something that almost made him cry with relief.

Silence. Complete merciful silence.

Black Jack spent the rest of the day trying to clean himself up. Nearly every inch of him was bruised and battered. His face was all torn up from the glass, the left eyeball nearly popped out of its socket. His sight had come back a little, but the eye was filled with blood, pus and blackened all around. Jack wasn't sure, but it felt like there was a good possibility that his nose was broken as well.

It was bad enough that the old geezer had been able to get the drop on him, but the worst part was that all of it was for nothing. No money, no jewelry, no nothing. A worthless old medal was all he had to show for a month of hard work.

He could never tell anyone about this, no way in hell. If word ever got out that the old man worked him over, he would never be able to hold up his head again. His career, maybe even his life, would be over. He laid back on the bed, too tired to even get undressed and closed his eyes for a moment, every part of him aching and sore.

The drumming whirl of a chopper flies overhead as he inches his way through the mud, trying to keep his head down. The jungle heat is overwhelming, the sweat blinding him as it runs in grimy tracks from underneath his helmet, straight into his eyes.

The mosquitoes are relentless, sharp pinches that assault his bare skin over and over. Up ahead he can hear rapid gunfire— pop-pop-pop—as he crawls along even faster, gritting his teeth with the effort.

Directly in front of him, the Greenhorn suddenly jumps up in a panic and begins to run. He knows that the area up ahead hasn't been swept for mines yet and the Greenhorn could be running straight into his death.

Without thinking, he leaps up and tackles the man as an earth-shattering explosion lifts them both high up into the air. They go down hard and he has just enough time to shield the Greenhorn with his own body as shards of razor-sharp shrapnel tear him to pieces.

If the Greenhorn would have taken one more step, he knows they would both be dead. He is bleeding from a thousand cuts, debris embedded in every part of him but he is grateful. They are both still alive, at least for now anyway.

Black Jack shot up in a cold sweat, the feel and taste of the nightmare still clinging to him. He could see with his one good eye what appeared to be welts all up and down his arms, angry-red and raw.

I am really falling apart, what the hell was that all about?

The details of the dream were so vivid that he swore he could still hear the gunfire, feel the sweltering heat of the jungle. Jack took a long pull from the whiskey bottle on his nightstand, the twenty or so ibuprofen from earlier in the evening not helping to ease the pain.

Where was I? Some war somewhere, in the Army? Instantly an angry voice ran through his head, coming out of nowhere:

"First Battalion, 5th Marines. Khe Sanh, Quang Tri Province, Vietnam. You asshole."

The hellish song began again, filling every corner of the room at an ear splitting volume. Black Jack hit the floor, pulling his gun out from beneath his pillow and waved it wildly in all directions. "All right, come out, you bastard!"

"Here's health to you and to our Corps, which we are proud to serve!"

"I'm right here, come out now!" Jack screamed into the empty room, "You want another shot at me old man?"

"In many a strife we've fought for life, and never lost our nerve!"

The music consumed every part of his head, louder and louder until Black Jack thought his brain would literally explode. He grabbed his head in his hands, shaking it wildly in all directions as his damaged eye began to bleed, hot red tears streaming down his face.

"What do you want from me? I killed you, fair and square old man! You need to stay dead!"

"If the Army and the Navy ever looked on Heaven's scenes!"

WHISTLING PAST THE VEIL

Jack had a sudden idea, grabbed the Purple Heart out of his pocket and held it high up into the air.

"Is this what you want?" he screamed in desperation as the song closed in, coming at him in waves from every direction. Jack began to laugh hysterically, swinging the medal like a lasso over his head and chucked it hard across the room.

"*They will find the streets are guarded by UNITED STATES MARINES!*"

The music continued to swirl around him in a volume he never even knew was possible. He had to be in hell, that was the only rational explanation. Jack blindly groped for his phone, hands shaking uncontrollably and managed to punch in 911.

"Please make it stop" he yelled into the phone, "Please get it out of here!"

The lights began to flicker on and off, the heinous demon choir taunting him as the sounds of gunfire whistled over his head, his nightmare actually brought to life. He fell to the ground, dragging his broken body inch by inch across the room with the Purple Heart looming large in his sight.

"OK, OK, I did it! I did it! I killed him!" Instantly, the music stopped. Black Jack began to laugh and cry at the same time, great heaving sobs that left him weak with relief. The Purple Heart was propped up against the wall, mocking him.

"You'll never beat me old man, medal or not!"

He dragged himself to his feet, giving the medal a large berth like it was some sort of poisonous snake. Jack stumbled into the kitchen in search of anything to stop the constant bleeding from his eye. He was in very bad shape, he really needed to go to a hospital but didn't dare risk it. He heard sirens in the distance, remembered that his cell phone was still connected to 911 and smashed it hard with his foot, grinding it into the carpet.

Damn it! Why did I call them? This shit is all in my head, I'd better get out of here quick.

He ran back out into the main room and threw some stuff in a bag, grabbing what little cash he had left and headed for the door. Making a snap decision, he picked up the Purple Heart, holding it out in front of his face and screamed out in a rage, one last time.

"You go to hell old man! Straight to hell and outta my head for good!"

All of a sudden, the music started up again, looping back to the very beginning. It assaulted him with its relentlessly familiar melody and Jack knew that even if he lived to be one-hundred, he would never, ever be able to forget it.

"From the halls of Montezuma, to the shores of Tripoli!"

Black Jack slowly set the Purple Heart down on the table and walked back into the kitchen, the song following right along with him.

"We will fight our country's battles, on the land and on the sea!"

He rummaged through a drawer until he found what he needed, cradling the items in his hands with relief.

"First to fight for right and freedom, and to keep our honor clean!"

Black Jack gently placed the ice pick in his left ear, lifted the hammer in his other hand, and drove it home.

Once, twice, three times. Just like hanging a picture nail, he laughed, easy-peasy lemon-squeezy!

As the blood started running down his neck, he calmly switched over to his other ear and began again.

"We are proud to claim the title of United States Marines!"

Black Jack screamed with maniacal laughter as the cops smashed through the front door, surrounding him with their guns drawn.

The last sound he heard, that he would ever hear, was the old man's evil song. The final verse of it swelled into a defiant climax, before slowly fading out into a complete and blissful silence.

Black Jack's days were simple now, he really didn't do much.

He was locked in a room most of the day, doctors and shrinks poking and prodding him at all hours. They found him criminally insane so they shipped him off to the booby hatch and threw away the key.

Black Jack didn't ever feel the need to talk to them for he was stone deaf and reveled in his cocoon of silence. Besides, who would ever believe him? He felt safe in here, where nothing was expected of him, passing his days in total peace in a place where there were no old men, medals, Marines or best of all—music.

"Not so fast asshole, you ain't heard nothin' yet!"

The voice went off like a cannon in his mind, completely shattering his tranquility. Black Jack couldn't hear it, but he could feel the scream coming up from the depths of his very soul as the song began to play once again, at full volume inside of his head.

He understood, way too late, the fatal mistake that better men than him had learned, the hard way, throughout the centuries. A mistake that would haunt him for the rest of his tortured, miserable life.

Alive or dead, don't ever, ever tangle with a United States Marine.

Originally published in "Dark Fire Fiction," 2017

Family Bible

He sat in the soft glow of candlelight, its shadow-flames dancing over the faces of his family proudly displayed on the wall beyond. He'd installed electric lights just a few years before, the very first home in the county to receive such a convenience. He knew that he would have no need of it now, never having been a man of excess.

As if to contradict his own nature, he reached across his desk to the crystal decanter on the oaken sideboard and poured himself two full fingers of single-malt bourbon. He would need the fortification in order to make it through the grim task that lay ahead. With a heart steeped in deep sorrow, John Clarence (J.C.) Torrington removed the thick family bible from the shelf and laid it out mournfully before him.

He'd spent his many years in continuous labor so that his wife and two daughters would have a life better than his own. He'd grown up hard and lean, a self-made man who'd scratched and fought his way through the Rocky Mountains, eventually finding a niche as a supplier and grocer for the endless line of miners and fortune seekers that crossed his path.

He and his wife Lizette had just celebrated thirty happy years together in the mining settlement of Leadville, Colorado. Both of them tending to the needs of the camp's prospectors, rising to prominence within the burgeoning community while steadily amassing their wealth.

Their good fortune, however, was tinged with heartbreak. Five years before, their eldest daughter Mary was struck down by influenza, one of the many plagues that sliced through the growing town like a scythe. J.C. and his wife ministered to their grown child around the clock, bringing in a team of doctors from Denver to try to save her. In the end, all of his success and wealth was for naught as she breathed her last in his arms, his wife wailing like a banshee in the room behind them.

J.C. threw himself even more into his work after Mary's death. He was the proprietor of three stores along Main Street and had interests in a dozen other businesses within the newly-formed town as well as several mining claims. Silver was king here, there was a booming, euphoric feel in the air. He'd decided to run for mayor, had just finalized his plans with Lizette and their surviving daughter, Mabel. He had everything a man of his means and distinguished years could possibly desire before the bottom fell out of his life once more—irrevocably and with complete finality.

J.C. threw back the bourbon in a single efficient arc, then quickly poured another. He lovingly ran his hand over the bible's cover, admiring the craftsmanship of the thick leather. This bible had been in his family for generations, an unbroken line of Torringtons stretching back well over a century. The pages were worn, reverently turned with a spattering of notes in the margins. He could envision his own great-grandfather in a similar pose, joyfully recording the birth of his first son, the first of many to be born in this rugged and freedom-blessed land. It was the clarion call of the west that had beckoned to his father and his father before him.

He traced the spidery script of his forebear, followed by his grandfather's precise writing. His own birth was recorded, and that of his two brothers followed by the dates of their tragic deaths on the blood-soaked battlefields of Gettysburg and Antietam. J.C. was the youngest and last surviving member of his family until his daughters graced the world with their enchanting, lively presence.

Mary and Mabel. Their names jumped out at him, written in his own firm hand directly beneath the entry of his and Lizette's wedding. Two birth dates confirming their existence, days that he counted amongst his happiest on earth. A shiver ran through him as he recalled writing in the date of Mary's demise, the clear memory of his hand faltering in its grim purpose causing a fresh jolt of grief to pierce his heart.

He had no further desire to be of this earth, his faith had been completely lost. He picked up his pen and slowly dipped it into the ink pot, summoning up the courage for what he needed to do. A single tear escaped his face and landed onto the page, causing the ink to blur as he carefully penned in the new dates. The candle flickered in the darkness, a physical gathering of grief and memory swirling around him as a second tear marred his efforts. J.C. was beyond caring, beyond any thought except that of completing his familial duty, the final record of a once vibrant family.

★

She perished in agony and blood as the child struggled to come. For endless hours she toiled in her labor, Lizette steadfastly by her side.

Mabel had married a fine young gentleman and moved to Denver the year before, J.C. and Lizette thrilling to the news that they would become grandparents in the spring. Lizette made the trip to the city to be with their daughter, J.C. intending to join them after the blessed event occurred.

He was hip-deep in work at his many enterprises, did not want to be in the way as he knew his wife would have things well in hand. He'd just boarded the coach and was on his way to them when the awful message came in over the wires, mere moments after his departure.

Mabel had eventually been delivered of a tiny baby girl. She lived for just past an hour longer, holding the babe in her arms before expiring. Lizette, in turn, softly cradled her only grandchild as the infant followed her mother into eternity, both of them appearing peaceful in their shared repose.

J.C. was tortured every night by the thought of his poor wife's state, that she was made to face such unspeakable tragedy alone. He was never to find out. Lizette died later that evening of a sudden heart attack in the room where her daughter and granddaughter were laid out, awaiting J.C.'s arrival.

The grandfather clock he'd special-ordered as a gift to his wife for their final anniversary chimed mournfully behind him. The bells tolled, one after the other, as J.C. etched his granddaughter's brief existence into the family bible. He never knew what Mabel would have called her so he simply wrote in *"Infant Girl"* underneath his beloved daughter's name. After recording the dark date he replenished the ink, hovering over his wife's entry before pausing to pour another dram.

A thousand memories assaulted him all at once. Lizette as she was on their wedding day, heartbreakingly beautiful with soft brown curls framing her porcelain face. The bell-like sound of her laughter as he twirled her around the empty wooden floorboards of their first modest home together. There she was again, radiant and serene presenting each one of her newborn babes out proudly for J.C.'s inspection.

His heart swelled with joy as he saw her there in their first store, bartering with the prospectors over goods like a seasoned old horse trader. He found her in his mind's eye, running through a mountain field of columbine with their growing girls, scooping up the delicate lavender flowers to place in one another's hair.

He'd never had a single moment of doubt in all of their years together that he had been truly blessed by the Almighty with his life's partner, he loved her beyond all time and reason. He could feel her in the darkened room with him now, the echo of her quiet strength moving his hand to complete her death entry before gently placing the pen onto the desk. JC had never before in his long life felt so weary, so bereft of purpose.

Another chime from the clock broke him out of his reverie. The house was as quiet as a tomb, a distant pop from somewhere outside providing the only clue that Leadville was still a raucous mining town. He had been a part of it's can-do spirit, setting out to conquer the town, but in the end, he and his family would be numbered among its vanquished.

J.C. allowed himself a final shot of bourbon before finishing his work for the evening. He had one more entry to write, wanted it to be clear and legible. He turned back a page to his own birth record, "*John Clarence Torrington, Son*" and added today's date and year, a record of his own death. He gently blew onto the fresh ink, satisfied that all was finally in order. His family legacy was complete. There would be no heirs to pass the family bible on to, but at least he had done his duty to them—there was some small comfort in that.

It was a fine legacy, indeed.

He reverently closed the bible and moved it back to its rightful place on the shelf, running his hand down its treasured spine in farewell. He drained the last of the bourbon while opening the drawer of his desk and extricating his revolver. His Remington was a part of his everyday existence, was a much needed precaution. J.C. counted himself fortunate that he'd never had to use it for its intended purpose, only occasionally to break up a drunken brawl here and there in the thoroughfare.

He was meticulous in its upkeep, cleaning it on a regular basis, making sure it was always loaded and at the ready. He had a strange, detached feeling as he placed the revolver up to his temple, cocked it, and prepared to join his family.

The click of the trigger was earth-shattering to his ear. He braced himself for the explosion, awaiting his violent transport into the afterlife, but nothing changed. He let out a long breath and tried anew, cursing himself for the error and advanced the cylinder.

Again, he pulled the trigger and received nothing but a hollow, unsatisfying click for his efforts. With shaking hands, he opened the cylinder and stared down in disbelief for there was not a single bullet to be found in any of the chambers.

Pausing for a brief moment, he looked in wonder at the revolver. It simply wasn't possible that it should be empty. He contemplated searching for the missing ammunition before deciding that the drink was finally catching up to him.

As if in a trance, J.C. slowly returned the gun to the drawer and blew out the candle. He went to his bed, giving himself up to some much- needed rest. In the end, he decided that the combination of grief and spirits had played tricks on his shattered mind.

There would be time to fulfill his destiny, he could put it off for another day.

As the clock struck twelve, a sudden, strong draft of cold air blew through the darkened room as J.C. took his leave, pushing the discarded bullets even farther back underneath Lizette's favorite settee where they would not be discovered until several years later.

It was upon that settee where she'd spent her happiest moments, her sewing in her lap as J.C. lingered at his desk and the girls sang and played together. She'd insisted upon the piano in the corner, right beneath the window where Lizette could play to her heart's content with the sun shining down upon the music and the glorious Rocky Mountains as a backdrop. A single note rang out from the piano as the strange gust of air faded away, returning the room to its natural state.

If J.C. would have been present at that very moment, he'd have been enveloped by a delicate scent of lavender. It floated on the remnants of the breeze—his wife's signature perfume—a testament to her memory and continued loving presence.

John Clarence Torrington was never to enact his self-destructive plan. Some years later, he met a lovely young woman on a train, thirty years his junior and made her his wife. His quiet home was renewed with life and laughter as several new Torringtons entered the world.

J.C. once again picked up his pen to record their joyful additions, certain that wherever Lizette was, she would be happy for him. He left his first death date exactly as it was, never wishing to revisit that dark chapter in his life.

The strange situation of J.C. having a much later second entry of death became an endless source of fascination to future family members when the dusty artifact was finally rediscovered in the attic of the family home.

They were very amused that their illustrious ancestor should be the only person in recorded history to have died twice. The old bible became a cherished heirloom, ensconced in its rightful place back on the shelf as J.C.'s many descendants all lived, loved and died within its timeworn pages.

Torrington family legend still holds that whenever a new addition is inscribed into the family bible, a mixed aroma of lavender and single-malt bourbon can be detected in the room. A fresh toast is then poured and raised to the family's continued success. Generations both seen and unseen all gather to celebrate in an unbroken line, standing together underneath the cathedral mountains of their Colorado home.

It was a fine legacy, indeed.

Originally published in "Edify Fiction," October 2017

Acceptance

Jack Gunderson was an asshole.

A first class, nickel-plated asshole for getting himself into this situation. He should have been more careful, should've never allowed his emotions to get in the way of his ultimate goal: vengeance. For that is what it was, if he was being completely honest with himself. Take away the satisfaction and thrill of executing a well constructed plan and that is what it all came down to. Pure, unadulterated revenge.

The old woman stared up at him, her sightless eyes accusing him from the great beyond, defiant even in death. At least he thought she was dead. After she'd hit the bottom he was sure he heard the fatal crunch, mortality finally asserting itself over the feisty old bird.

She'd fought him ferociously in the end—her knotted, arthritic finger nearly blinding him as she stomped down hard on his foot causing Gunderson to bellow and lash out in a purple rage. He hurtled her down the stairs much harder than he'd intended after that final indignity, only to trip over her goddamned cat and fall ass-over-teakettle right behind her.

Definitely not part of his plan.

He'd allowed his heart to rule over his head; and that was how he found himself there at the bottom of the staircase, unable to move, with a dead woman at his feet.

A bona-fide, certified asshole was Jack Gunderson. There was absolutely no doubt about it.

If he could move at that moment, put pen to paper, or even flip on his recording device what an amazing story he would tell, for Jack Gunderson fancied himself a writer. A bestselling author if only he could catch that one big break and get his foot in the door.

Standing at the threshold of fifty-years old, Jack had spent years writing and trying to publish his work. Novels and short stories, essays, novellas and even the occasional poem or two were lovingly crafted and submitted to various places with mixed results. He had a few credits to his name, but true success eluded him at the one place that Gunderson was convinced would finally jump-start his career: an organization run by one Mrs. Frank Wentworth-Theme, chief editor and soul-crusher extraordinaire of the Wentworth-Theme Publishing House.

Jack always kept a stack of rejection letters piled high on his desk for posterity, left over from the olden days when he would actually send in his manuscripts via snail mail. The rejection letters from Mrs. Theme were special.

He hung each one onto his office wall, puncturing them over and over again with sharp-tipped darts as he began to hatch his plan of revenge. The fact that they papered the entirety of the room like "Jack Gunderson's Grooveyard of Forgotten Favorites" only increased his indignant fury as the years passed by.

"Dear Mr. Gunderson, I regret to inform you..." always followed by an unflinchingly harsh opinion of exactly what she thought of his writing. Each time she would send back his battle-worn manuscript scarred by her merciless pen, the pages covered in blood-red ink.

Gunderson pictured the woman as a viper, a blood-sucking parasite who had married into her situation and browbeaten her ancient husband into a premature grave. He was certain that the poor man went willingly in an attempt to escape her relentless harping, as any respectable man still in nominal possession of his balls would do.

Mrs. Theme took over the family empire after the old fart croaked, becoming a hard-nosed business woman and steadfast barrier to Gunderson's lifelong ambitions. In Jack's mind, she alone held the key to make or break an up-and-coming author like himself.

Wentworth-Theme published everything under the sun from novels, magazines and newspapers to ezines, blogs and even old lady critique circles. They published everything, that is, except for anything that Jack Gunderson submitted.

As the rejections kept piling up, Gunderson began to fixate more and more on Mrs. Theme, blaming her as the source of his every failure and bout of writer's block. Eventually he stopped writing altogether, convinced that his creativity had been sucked out of him by the vampiric old harpy. He knew that he was slowly losing his mind, could feel it slipping farther away with every missile he chucked at those tattered old letters on the wall.

Jack constantly obsessed about what the old lady had against him, refusing to believe that it could actually have anything to do with the quality of his writing.

No, that simply wasn't possible. Mrs. Theme had it out for him, there really was no other explanation. It was the least he could do to return the favor.

Gunderson attempted to shift his weight on the stair, leaving him with a shooting pain running along his backside for the trouble. Something was seriously wrong with him.

He thought at first it might be his leg until he began to lose all sensation in his right arm. He knew that he had fallen badly, was twisted up like a pretzel with his considerable six-foot-four frame sprawled out onto the stairs like a drunken college student.

The late afternoon sun fell into disarray, leaving Gunderson and Mrs. Theme alone together in the first shadows of evening. Jack felt a sudden jolt of fear remembering that Mrs. Theme had no immediate family. No children or friends that might come to check in on her. He could be stuck here a very long time.

Stuck here, with her.

He took a deep, calming breath as dusk fell over the stairs and heard a sudden noise below him in the gathering darkness. An angry hissing sound, raising the hairs on the back of his neck as he entertained the sickening possibility that Mrs. Theme might not be dead after all.

Mrs. Theme had retired a few years ago, living in a modest suburban house that Gunderson knew was way below her considerable means. He'd been studying her for years, knew that she was a frugal old bat that still had the first dollar she'd ever made. It wasn't hard to figure out her routine, one horrific boring day bleeding into the next as she went about her colorless dotage.

It was no big deal to break in, Gunderson was surprised at how little security the scion of the Wentworth-Theme dynasty actually had. In a way, he felt sorry for her. Alone in the house every day with no one to visit with, no family or friends. She was the last survivor of her era, at least until Jack came to call. She should have been grateful for the company, should've wanted to grovel at his feet for the mortal sin of destroying his career.

As it was, he never even got the chance to state his many grievances. She robbed him of even that final satisfaction. The old hellcat viciously attacked him at the very moment he broke in through the back window.

They fought down the length of the hallway, the elderly woman surprisingly resilient, finally ending up at the basement staircase. A steep, winding monstrosity where Gunderson now found himself trapped with a corpse, his dreams of revenge becoming shattered as his body also appeared to be.

Jack awoke from a light, disturbing doze as the first traces of an odor began to permeate the air. Mrs. Theme was most definitely dead. Her various bodily functions kept going off like a deranged symphony, causing jolts of adrenaline to shoot through him at every fresh, hideous sound. He could hear the pops and hisses as the body settled into decrepitude and began to mottle. It was like something that had sat out a bit too long in the sun, a ripe, meaty smell that caused him to dry heave as he struggled to keep it together.

Christ, I need to get out of here. Broken leg or not, I am not staying down here with her in the dark.

If he lifted his head straight up in a painful arc, he could just about make out the top of the first stair. He estimated that he needed to hoist himself up about ten full steps before he could somehow get over the landing to his freedom.

He rested his head back down, smelling traces of her demonic cat's urine in the carpet fibers. If he ever got out of this, he swore he would pay that fucking cat one of his special visits as well.

Gunderson decided to take himself for a test run as a low, guttural sound caused large goose flesh to pop out all over his arms. He knew it was just the dead body doing its macabre work, but his imagination was beginning to run wild as the otherwise silent house fell deeper into night. He was a writer after all, it went with the territory.

He scrunched up his nerve and used his one good arm as a lever, placing his right knee as high as he could manage onto the stair above and dragging his worthless left leg along like a side of beef. A surge of molten-hot agony greeted his effort, causing Jack to scream in frustration.

After what felt like a superhuman burst of energy, his useless limbs finally came along for the ride as he made it up to the next stair, collapsing in sheer exhaustion. Stair by stair, hour by hour he moved along, an inch at a time, as the body continued to sing its horrific tune below. Mrs. Theme appeared to be mocking him in her decay, getting in the last word from beyond the grave.

He lost all sense of time and place, his entire world reduced to the urine-stained steps, moving along at a glacial pace. He slept off and on when the pain became too much to bear, the house plunging into complete blackness as he labored. He could sense that he was near the end, the distance between him and Mrs. Theme growing blessedly greater with every painful movement. With cold sweat streaming into his eyes, Jack threw his hand over the coveted top stair, feeling around for some sort of purchase. *Success at last, thank God!*

At that exact moment, the devil cat jumped out and attacked his scrabbling hand. It pounced upon him with sharp claws, placing a vicious bite deep into the webbed skin between Jack's thumb and index finger. Gunderson bellowed in pain and fear, wildly waving the beast away as he fell hard, back down every single step, landing painfully at the bottom. He accidentally kicked the body of Mrs. Theme, causing it to erupt into a fresh batch of ghastly music. He could feel his bare arm resting up against its cold, lifeless flesh.

Gunderson screamed until his throat went hoarse, finally falling into a black, self preserving sleep as the night wore on and the cat went off in search of its next victim.

The first signs of liquid daybreak were streaming through the upstairs windows, casting a putrid yellow hue on the walls above. Jack noted that the basement stairs were still cool and dark, the lower level being the last to ever see the sun. His throat was on fire with a searing thirst, his body weak and aching with hunger pangs. Every inch of him was battered and bruised, ranging from a dull ache to burning anguish in his broken leg. He knew that he would need to try the stairs again, didn't know if he could even summon up the energy for another attempt.

He tried to move his good arm, searching for the clammy flesh of the cadaver. He could certainly smell her all around him, it was overpowering and filled with rot and death, making every inhalation of breath a chore. He moved the arm again, finding nothing but empty space. He could hear it then, a scraping sound like someone behind him sharpening a knife on a stone.

"Hello? Hello, help! Help me! I am down here! Please!"

Jack waited for a response, no longer afraid that he would be caught and thrown into jail for murder, no longer caring about anything in the world but survival. A low, menacing hum greeted his plea, muffled like someone trying to sing through a mouthful of wet earth. Jack could feel the wetness spreading through his groin, his bladder giving up the fight as the scraping continued directly behind him, louder and louder as it approached. The humming was slightly off key, overly bright. Like the song of a lunatic. Or a crazy old woman. Jagged, raspy breathing reached his ears, his nightmare shambling across the basement floor and onto the bottom stair.

Gunderson screamed as an icy, dead hand reached out and roughly grabbed his ankle, pulling him deep into the bowels of the basement and off of the accursed stairs.

"Dear Mr. Gunderson, I regret to inform you that you have been accepted at last," the creature that had been Mrs. Theme croaked into his ear, her hot, rancid breath making Jack's eyes water as her other hand wrapped itself around his neck.

"Finally. Forever and ever."

Acceptance, Jack thought in dark wonder, what every writer dreams of. I am finally accepted!

It was his final euphoric thought as Mrs. Theme efficiently liberated his head from his neck. Off it came in a great crimson flourish, drenching the basement in blood and bits of gore as Gunderson's discarded body twitched and buckled about on the concrete floor.

Her grim work at an end, Mrs. Theme danced his head around the basement in childlike abandon, eager and ready for their long and fruitful collaboration to finally begin.

Originally published in "Dark Fire Fiction," 2017

Bed Bath and Way Beyond

Darkness.

He sees nothing, feels nothing but the pitch black of cool oblivion. From a great distance he can hear a rumbling, a jumble of noise that he can't quite place. It is all around him now, a tremor that works it's way up from the depths beneath him into his very being.

What am I? Where am I?

A brief flash of recognition begins and passes before he can catch it....a glimpse of a face, beautiful, framed in a bonnet... the sound of heavy wheels on uneven land...laughter, light and lyrical comes unbidden like music to his ears as a great burst of light explodes into his vision. Brighter than anything he could ever imagine, it jolts him out of his reverie and drops him back into the blackness. And he is grateful.

He sleeps without dreaming until that incessant, constant rumbling slowly brings him back. From somewhere a sound blares into his head, loud and terrifying like opening the gates of hell....

What is that? Where am I?

He can feel his pulse quicken, a cold sweat overtaking him. In his mind's eye he sees her, hears her gentle voice call out to him...Elizabeth...small children running across the open prairie, their blond hair shining in the sun...a mountain vista rises before him filling him with awe.

Jeremiah! Awaken my love-the daylight beckons.

Jeremiah? Is that who I am?

The constant humming gets louder and he can feel its pulse throughout his body, making him rise back into the light. He sees her again, beautiful, reaching out to him-Elizabeth.

Of course, how could he ever forget?

Her delicate features and tiny stature concealing an iron will, a formidable character. Who else could get him to pack up and follow a dream thousands of miles across the great plains?

Trust in the Lord, Jeremiah, and He will provide. I am Jeremiah. Jeremiah Graves.

The realization hits him like a burst of cold water. Elizabeth. Marjorie, William, Charles....he sees his wife, each of his children smiling at him in turn. He hears the bellow of an ox, a dog barking. He feels the sun on his face and smells the rosewater scent of his wife.

I am Jeremiah Graves from Lancaster, Pennsylvania, and I am seeking a new beginning, freedom on the open frontier for myself and my family.

Suddenly an unbearable blast of sound jolts him from his rest and spits him out into a dark, cold night upon a hill of dirt.

Frantically, he leaps to his feet. His shoes come apart, shards of leather flying off into the night. His first sensation is extreme dizziness as he falls to his knees and tries desperately to make sense of his surroundings. His eyes, long accustomed to complete darkness, try to adjust. Flashes of rapid light dance across his vision.

There it is again!

Sounds burst past him from every direction like a barrage of terrifying waves in a deranged symphony. He lies back on the hard dirt and looks up to the heavens, tries to catch his breath. A spidery cloud slides by revealing an enormous blood-red moon in the night sky. A spattering of stars, constellations he vaguely remembers, can be seen through the haze.

What is that smell? Where on earth am I?

On the wind he faintly hears the voice of his wife calling out to him.

Jeremiah!

Jeremiah feels her fingers gently caress his cheek then jolts up when the sensation is revealed to be a fat, wriggling worm. Trying to scream, he is flummoxed when only a hoarse scratch comes out along with a mouthful of damp earth.

He closes his eyes and tries to summon her, find her in that comforting darkness but he is utterly alone, completely bereft.

I am Jeremiah Graves. I am Jeremiah Graves he repeats over and over as the horrific sounds continue to speed past him.

Elizabeth my love, are you there? Has God forsaken me? Is this hell?

His fingers claw the ground as he scrabbles back up and tries to stand. Out of nowhere a large, monstrous object roars across the sky trailing a line of bright, white smoke. Jeremiah screams, the sound finally breaking free in a hideous wail.

Falling back to the ground, he rolls down the hill and straight into the husk of a dead tree. He looks to the top of the hill and barely makes out the shapes there.

Headstones? Am I in a graveyard?

He ducks and covers his head as the flying monster passes directly above him then mercifully, out of sight.

One, two, ragged breaths calm him as he tries to collect his thoughts.

A graveyard? How can this be?

An overwhelming sadness washes over him as a distant memory tugs at his mind. A tiny cross lovingly placed alongside a desolate stretch of land. Elizabeth, inconsolable, wracked with sobs. William. His own beloved Willy sleeping forever in the prairie grass.

An earth shattering crash nearby slams him back to reality and sends him hurtling over the wrought iron fence into...

At first glance, he is convinced he has descended into utter madness.

The scene unfolds before him, assaulting his every sense with unflinching disbelief.

What sorcery is this? What horror!

Harsh yellow lights come at him from every direction, dozens of false suns encased in glass. *What manner of fire is this that does not flicker?*

Giant wooden poles the height of twenty men tower above him holding wires that crackle and hum like devil's tails. Bright, enormous words jump out at him in unearthly hues he has never before seen. Garish, unnatural colors on dozens of sprawling structures that make his eyes water as he tries to read them.

He finally discovers the source of the ghastly sounds as it barrels towards him in the night. A great steel monster heads straight for him with two eyes of supernatural light, rendering him immobile with fright. The hellish cacophony of sounds, unbearably loud and jarring, fill his head as the creature bears down to attack him.

At the last possible moment, he manages to break free of it's evil spell just seconds before it can strike. He can feel the demon's breath as it passes, emitting an earth-shattering scream in a tone he never knew existed. As he watches it pass he could swear he saw a man in it's giant glass belly, a chariot driven perhaps by Satan himself.

The spell broken, he begins to run, jamming his unclad feet onto a strange blackened surface that cuts at him. But wait! There are hundreds of these demon chariots, speeding together in an unbroken line, belching out their infernal smoke like dragon's fire. They are everywhere, an unending mobile army marching through the night. He runs past sleeping chariots, still creatures that lie in wait for their evil passengers. He does not wish to disturb their slumber and risk their wrath so he runs until he feels his lungs must burst.

For the first time he notices that his clothes are moldering and falling away with every step. Bony white fingers poke through what used to be his Sunday best and he realizes in wonderment that those are his actual bones jutting out of the rotting suit.

Nononono!

He tentatively reaches out, touches his face....

Before his mind can react a giant golden dog leaps into his line of vision, pink jeweled leash dragging behind, followed by the stunned face of a woman transfixed in horror. He pivots back as the creature lunges for him. Maniacal barks fill the air and temporarily drown out the demon chariots.

He has a fleeting remembrance of his children playing with a young pup as they weave in and out of the legs of an unamused team of oxen.

Where are they now, my precious children? The two remaining, my one in heaven? Where is my love, my Elizabeth?

He prays fervently that they are nowhere in this strange world, that he has been the one transported to hell and not them. He feels a tear fall across his exposed skull and wonders how it is still possible for him to cry.

Up ahead he can see the graveyard as he dodges sleeping chariots and the few passersby that gape at him in open astonishment. He briefly notes that the women are all wearing men's trousers and all of them hold up square objects that they pull from their pockets. The citizens of hell eagerly watch his macabre dance as parts of Jeremiah begin to come apart and fly off in different directions.

He barely manages to vault the iron fence as the dog slams into it at full speed. He lands hard and watches what was once his left leg fly back through the iron bars. He begins to crawl, praying his arms will hold out just a little while longer.

The sounds of barking, excited voices follow him from behind but he is not deterred. He knows where he must go, perhaps he has known all along...

Joan Claire could hardly wait to shut off the lights and lock up for the night. Her shift is at an end and it has been a very long day. It is "All Hallows Eve." Seriously, who wants to buy matching sheets or a foam body pillow on a night like tonight?

She has a date for the first time in awhile and she has just enough time to shower and change before heading to the party. She pulls out her cell phone and briefly scans her texts-yep Kyle was all set to pick her up in an hour.

She pulls the keys from her jeans and heads for the door. The neon white "Bed, Bath and Beyond" sign angrily buzzes and sputters. One of these days the manager is going to have to fix that, it is extremely annoying.

Joan locks the door behind her and turns to look, as she always does, at the odd little cemetery in the parking lot of the Pioneer Hills Shopping Center.

It is the strangest thing-the family that sold the land for the shopping center had one unique provision: the little pioneer cemetery must remain exactly where it has been for over 150 years. They did not want to disturb the graves of their ancestors so the lot was fenced off intact, the concrete jungle sprouting up all around it.

It sits right behind the Chic-Fil-A, across the way from the Bed, Bath and Beyond and the rest of the homogenous shops that can be seen in every strip mall across the country.

Joan sighs-the cemetery seems so forlorn in this endless sea of parking lots. A physical reminder of a simpler time, maybe a better one...she shelves the uninvited wistful feeling and turns towards her car when she sees a sight that has to be some sort of a prank.

A large Golden Retriever has escaped from it's owner right outside of the PetSmart and appears to be chasing a skeleton wearing rags at full speed across the parking lot.

The rare blood moon shines down upon this eye popping scene as pieces of the skeleton begin to fall off inciting the dog even further.

What the?

Joan's first reaction is instantaneous-she snaps up her phone and hits the record button.

Is this the set of a Halloween movie? Some kind of Youtube joke?

The cemetery did attract a few oddballs during nights like this-this has to be something good! She is able to catch it all the way to where the amazingly limber set of bones flies over the fence and into the darkness of the graveyard beyond.

The last shot she takes is of the Golden Retriever happily prancing off with what looks to be a femur bone.

Man, I'm glad I got that! Who would ever believe me?

She gets into her car and drives off to do what all good teenagers do-share the amazing video with everyone on all of her social media accounts.

Jeremiah knows that his time is short as he continues to crawl his way back through the lonesome graveyard.

He can hear them even louder now as he approaches his final, and hopefully eternal, destination. Even knowing, the shock of seeing it takes what is left of his breath away.

"Jeremiah Graves, 1800-1865"

Pictures of his long life dance before him. Elizabeth in her wedding gown of lace, Marjorie taking her first steps in the prairie flowers, Charlie's deep blue eyes-the very image of his mother.

And Willy. His fair haired little boy, sitting upon his knee as he passes the reins of the oxen over to him and they lead them forth to begin their incredible journey. Together as a family, all of them as one.

Papa, papa! Like the sweetest music he has ever heard and then she is there... waiting for him, they all are. Their loving embrace welcomes him home as he falls head first into his open grave.

And he is grateful.

Originally published in "Dark Fire Fiction," 2016

Cooking, With Dogs

The old man felt the sun on his wizened face, warm and full of promise. He could smell the thin mountain air of his Colorado childhood as he breathed in deeply, holding it in as long as he could. God, *I had forgotten how good it felt to take a deep, full breath. I am home, finally home at last!*

He had recently celebrated his 125th birthday and while that age was fairly common with the technology of the 2100's, it was still a very distinguished number.

I have lived a wonderful life, he thought, my family, my life's work. A sudden bark in the distance pulled him back to his surroundings. Wait! I am having the dream again!

Every night, it seemed, he would come here in his dreams, a memory mixed with longing. The path before him was dusty and he swore he could taste the grit in his teeth as a large Labrador retriever raced past him chasing a ball. We used to come here all the time, he mused, my parents, sisters and me, every spring when the weather changed, we would return...

With the unique freedom of a dream, he began to run down the well worn path he knew so well. His legs flew with an abandon he hadn't felt in decades as a pair of large, mahogany Irish setters matched him step for step. He looked around and saw the untouched land of the old Colorado plains. Trees were just beginning to bud, tall prairie flowers flourished in a brilliant purple as the afternoon sun shone down on the snow covered mountains.

He heard the whinny of a horse coming from the old stable on the hill. How he had rejoiced when he took his first riding lesson there! How old was he then—nine, ten? Nigh on one-hundred-fifteen years ago. He searched his memory trying to recall the name of this magical place, what was it? Cherry Creek, yes that was it. It was a parcel of protected prairie land right by his house that included a man-made reservoir and a very special place where people could let their dogs run free.

He turned the corner and saw a purebred German shepherd running alongside a black, full-sized poodle. A snow white husky with one blue eye vied for his attention as he reached out to stroke its silky fur. He felt pure, unadulterated joy as he reached the bank of the small creek just knowing what awaited him there.

He had accomplished so many things in his long life, he thought wistfully, recalling his childhood. Ah, the joys of being a boy! A hundred memories danced across his mind all at once, running, jumping, sports, sticks and mud pies, taunting his two big sisters—those carefree days. His mother in the kitchen, taking a large, brown turkey out of the oven. *Is that when I first discovered that cooking was in my blood, the moment my life's ambition took shape?*

His father would bring him to wrestling tournaments every weekend in the spring and coach his football team in the fall. God, how I've missed them, he thought as he pictured himself as he was then. Tall for his age, blond hair and skinned knees. A spattering of freckles across his nose that would get darker every summer whether he liked it or not. His mother was always complaining that he had a dirty face that would never go away, no matter how many times she would try clean it. He chuckled as he remembered her exasperation. I would always duck just in time and the dirt would stay. I was constantly moving then, a super-boy, unstoppable!

He pictured himself as a teenager, jumping up and catching the ball mid-air as he ran into the end zone for the touchdown. The crowds cheering, the proud expression on his father's face. The first time he made the perfect souffle at cooking class, just beginning his dream of becoming a chef. My parents weren't sure about it at the time, but they had no idea that it would turn out so well, none of us did.

He served in the military, he recalled proudly, ten-mile marches every morning followed by peeling hundreds of potatoes in the mess, the Army preferring to do things the old-fashioned way. It was good training, he thought, reminding him of the basics—something every good chef needed to remember.

A white flash darted past him, pulling him out of his reverie. God, that's a Greyhound—look at him run! The old man rounded the corner, just past the second switchback and saw it once again, in all of it's glory. The creek was high this time, he noted, the dream was never exactly the same way twice. The water flowed at a decent clip as dozens of happy dogs frolicked and played, a true canine paradise. He saw a chocolate lab swim after a ball as a short, stubby dachshund attempted to steal it away. Every kind of dog he could ever imagine was represented, every color and size. His old eyes feasted upon the happy scene.

God, that's exactly how it was! He could almost see himself there as the boy he was then, pants rolled up, shoes thrown to the side as he stood knee deep in the water with his favorite stick in hand. The skilled conductor of his very own canine symphony.

A tiny Chihuahua darted between his legs and ran off before he could even react. A large pack of dogs broke away and began to run at a full gallop. Just then, he heard two loud barks as a gorgeous rough collie raced onto the scene, a classic Lassie dog, and began to form the unruly group into a large moving herd...Could it be? His heart began to race, he knew this dog, he was sure of it. He cupped his hands around his mouth and yelled out in a booming voice, a voice, he noticed, that was much younger than his own ancient one: "Thunder! Thunder, come here boy!"

He remembered those early days in culinary school fresh out of the service, working in kitchens all over Denver as he learned his craft one recipe at a time.

"Your grandfather was a marvelous cook," his mother would tell him on his visits home, both of them working in the kitchen together.

"He'd always say: if you can read, you can cook" and that was possibly the best advice he had ever received.

He read up plenty on all of the great chefs, tweaking as he went, experimenting and adding on to their well-loved recipes. On the day he graduated, his mother handed him an old, battered box, well worn from years of use. It was his grandfather's recipe collection and it became his most prized possession. It never left his sight as he began to add his own recipes and creations into it, the generations coming together in perfect culinary harmony.

On the day he set out for the world, his mother cried and his father firmly shook his hand, both of them standing huddled together, arms around each other as he ran to catch his flight. Everything he owned was stowed in a beat up Army duffel bag on his back, clothes being secondary to his spices, knife roll and ever present recipe box.

He landed in Amsterdam the following day, filled with excitement and eager to set out. Walking past the famed Red Light District, he turned over the possibilities of his new life over in his mind, what he would do, where he would go. He had no plan. Just his Army bag and an all encompassing desire to cook. Bored, over painted women beckoned to him through the windows, wounded butterflies encased in glass as he moved past them, not wanting any distraction to lead him away from his goals.

A journeyman cook, a wandering spirit, he never stayed in any one place for very long. He would literally go to the ends of the earth and back for the perfect spice, the rarest and most delectable flavor combinations. He had no roots, no one holding him back.

The next four years were spent in Europe, traveling from country to country, stopping to work along the way. He would take any job he could get in the kitchen, making sure to closely observe the chefs, sous chefs and line cooks as they practiced their craft. He began to view cooking as a real art form, playing around with presentation and creative ways to bring his dishes to life. When they would let him, he would take over the preparation and plating, using asymmetrical shapes and bright, vibrant colors.

The time-honored rule had always been that the plate had to be arranged like a clock with specific food types placed at certain hours. You could find carbs at eleven o'clock, protein at six, vegetables at another hour, all of the food groups represented like an edible clock. He turned that notion completely on its head, stacking different foods in all sorts of combinations, the stranger the better.

His dishes began to look like paintings. It was said that his cuisine was placed like Picasso, flavored like Van Gogh with sauces strewn across the plate like a Jackson Pollock painting. His dishes dazzled the eyes as well as the taste buds of the diners everywhere he went. He began to get a following, the early age of social media in those days following his every exploit, his travels to each new restaurant. His followers eventually gave him a name, one that stuck with him throughout all the years of his storied career, try as he might to ignore it.

He was simply called "The Artisan."

He was cooking at a small Italian bistro when he found his first traveling companion. The dog was scrawny and dirty, eating scraps from the dumpster behind the building when the Artisan came upon him. He was a rat terrier with one brown eye, hungry and wild. He was instantly smitten, holding out a veal cutlet to the dog, slowly gaining his trust. The dog came back the next day and the day after that, wagging his tail as soon as the Artisan came out. On the fourth day he brought him home and named him Sammy. They were inseparable after that, man and dog, traveling the continent together, as the Artisan plied his trade. He would never in his life be without a dog again.

The collie broke away and barreled toward him, his long hair flying in the wind, splashing water in his wake like a scene from an old technicolor movie.

"Thunder, is it really you?" he cried as the dog knocked him over in his joy, gleefully licking his face. Miraculously, the fall didn't hurt his old bones at all. The man doubled over in laughter as Thunder continued to enthusiastically slobber all over him.

Thunder was his sister's dog, he remembers some ninety-five+ years ago now? He lost both of his sisters a few years back and thought that the trouble with great age was being the only one left, the last testament to people and a world that lived on only in dreams. Then of course, there was her. Always her. The one great love of his life. He can just see her in his mind's eye, her golden hair shining in the sun, the most beautiful woman he had ever seen.

He was building quite a reputation as a young chef who wandered the world in those days, always with his faithful dog. For awhile he and Sammy traveled with a pair of entertainers, brothers who worked as a living statue mime and juggler on the street in every major city they went to. Pietro and Jacques filmed their little group's every exploit and trip, adding to his already considerable social media exploits, giving the Artisan an ongoing platform they laughingly called "Cooking, with Dogs."

They would film him on an old device they used to call a "smart phone," the one item even traveling vagabonds had to have in those long ago days. They would capture him preparing gourmet meals alongside of the road with fresh ingredients from the local markets, a portable propane stove and crackling fire, chronicling the rapport between chef and dog in each new exotic locale. Sammy would dance around for the camera, begging for a taste of each new creation, flipping up in the air like a seasoned performer. The Artisan always suspected their popularity was due more to Sammy than to himself, but their viewers continued to increase with every new posting. An "internet sensation" they called it back then, as people would try to track him down, get a picture with Sammy or sample one of his dishes.

With the amount of the attention he was getting, he really had no trouble when it came to the ladies. Nearly every evening he and his traveling companions could be found in the company of a variety of young women, starry eyed and beautiful under the intoxicating moonlight. The Artisan never gave any of them very much thought, allowing his over-eager friends to bask in the limelight while he continued to practice his craft. They were all impossibly young, he chuckled softly in his sleep, young and living in the moment.

They lived their lives on the road as he continued to ply his trade wherever he could find a position while "Cooking,

With Dogs" consumed his every spare moment. He thought they would go on like that forever as their group reached the "City of Light," the place where their shared road would finally come to an end. Jacques and Pietro were headed to the Eiffel Tower while the Artisan was hoping to learn the secrets of the masters, the greatest chefs in the world who all gathered there. He was so excited that he could hardly sleep the night before, dreaming of all the places he would go, the knowledge he would gain. The very last thing he ever expected to do was to fall in love, even in a city so renowned for it.

He had absolutely no interest in romance, other than of the culinary kind. So of course, that's exactly when it found him. Or rather, his faithful dog Sammy found it for him.

The Artisan remembered that fateful day in the shadow of the Eiffel Tower when Sammy broke away and ran up to an exquisite young woman, tail wagging, refusing to leave her side until he came over and introduced himself. *God bless that dog, how smart he was!*

Every part of his being was instantly entranced as he approached her, slowly willing his feet to move as every instinct told him to run away. She had eyes the color of the sky he noticed, large and intelligent as he struggled to find something, anything to say. Sammy wove back and forth between his feet, leading him closer to her. He saw his friends out of the corner of his eye as they worked the square, smiling with curiosity as to who she was. Most likely wondering how they had missed making her acquaintance themselves.

He never knew why, but she agreed to have coffee with him as they sat overlooking the Champs-Elysees, Sammy curled up at his feet. He couldn't believe his own great luck. She was an absolute vision, witty and kind. He was surprised to find out that she was an American, the irony of fate dancing across his mind. She was from eastern Iowa she said, had come to Paris after college to follow her dreams of becoming an artist. She used color on her canvas like he created his dishes; bright and vibrant landscapes, bold portraits and gentle brushstrokes adding to the flavor of any subject.

They talked for hours and the Artisan somehow knew that his life would never be the same again. She traveled with him after that, the two of them forming a kind of vagabond family with Sammy leading the way. In Milan, they picked up another stray, a Black Lab named Bonnie who added her playful antics to their ongoing blog. She took over the filming as he continued to create, completely engrossed in each new dish as the dogs romped and played all around him. It was a magical time, the two of them so much in love, each day an adventure.

They married in the spring at a little chapel in the French countryside, Jacques and Pietro standing witness to their vows. A dog stood, one next to the bride and one by the groom as they pledged their lives to each other. She covered every inch of their tiny newlywed apartment with landscapes and portraiture. For a wedding gift she presented him with a painting of two very special dogs, one all black, and one with a patch of brown over one eye. That painting still hung in his room today, a physical reminder of those early, star-crossed days.

He was apprenticed to a chef in Barcelona when she announced that they were expecting their first child. He immediately began to look to the future, deciding that the time was finally right to pack up and move back to the states. He brought them home to Colorado, introducing her to his excited family, both of his parents insisting that they renew their vows in front of their family and friends. They found a little house with a yard for the dogs and got ready to welcome their first baby.

The Artisan worked all over metro Denver, the bustling "Lo-Do" scene downtown a hot spot for fine dining in those days. After their daughter was born he began to really contemplate the future, realizing that his lifelong dream was to finally open his own restaurant. They scrimped and saved, giving up "Cooking, With Dogs" and focusing completely on their shared goal. She was right there alongside him when they opened the doors, her paintings and bold color schemes welcoming in new diners while his tantalizing spices wafted through the air. It needed a name that fit both of them so they simply called it "Canvas" and set about to offer their patrons an unforgettable and artistic dining experience. He took his years of experience from his many travels and put them all to use in his cooking, serving international dishes in his own unique style. The Artisan was truly home at last.

As their family grew from three to four to five, he worked tirelessly at his craft as Canvas grew in popularity and renown. People would still ask about the dogs from his internet days, both Sammy and Bonnie aging happily right along with their growing family. As the years went by, they had to say goodbye one by one to their loyal friends, the hardest part of their lives together. Their three children would always remember dogs being part of their family at every stage of their lives, growing up with the stories of their parents' storied romance and "Cooking, With Dogs."

After some years, he received his first Michelin Star and was classified as a "Rising Star," meaning that his profile was going up and more Stars would most likely follow. Canvas was filled to capacity every night, the hottest place in town. He began to consider opening another restaurant, eager to begin branching out as more accolades and reviews came pouring in.

His family was thriving as well, quickly outgrowing their first place together. He was highly successful by the time they moved, taking their three family dogs with them into their new, more spacious home.

He had his third Michelin Star and three restaurants under his belt when he decided to try something a little different. He found a place right on the Sixteenth Street Mall downtown, with a large open patio. As the diners gathered outside in the nice weather, he created a second patio right next door allowing the diners to keep their dogs with them in a safe, clean and separate enclosure. He even had a small doggy menu that the owners could choose for their pets, people and dogs all gathered together. His kids were hired to take care of the dogs while the patrons dined, walking them and catering to their every need. It was a huge hit, beyond anything he had ever experienced as people poured in, excited at the novelty. It was the most casual of his restaurants, but the one that ended up being closest to his heart. It reminded him of his earlier days in Europe, Sammy and Bonnie and his one true love. In a nod to his earlier life he called it "Eating, With Dogs" and there was never an empty table in the house.

As their kids grew up and moved away, he and his love rediscovered each other. She had spent years as a successful painter in her own right, decorating all of their businesses and selling pieces here and there. He knew that he would never have had such tremendous success without her. They had been married almost fifty years when he took her back across the sea, stopping at each place that they had traveled to all those years before.

He made time to confer with colleagues in the culinary world, revisiting all of the places where he'd once cooked and working in their kitchens as a visiting chef. They spent over a year on sabbatical, branching out from Europe and stopping in Asia to visit master chefs there. Afterwards, they went on an African safari and ended up "down under" in Australia for a month. It took a lot of red tape, but they managed to bring home another stray dog, an Australian Shepherd, from a local shelter there.

In the end, they had almost seventy years together. With their three kids, countless grandchildren, a few greats with even one great-great thrown in, it was all a very grand adventure. He was well into his eighties before he even gave a thought to winding down, finding that the demands of working full time were getting to be too much for his physical abilities. When he finally did retire, he began writing. Recipes, cookbooks and an autobiography fittingly called, "Cooking, With Dogs." It chronicled the highs and lows of a life well-lived and through it all there were dogs, always dogs.

He remembered another night, years later, holding her hand, tears streaming down his face as he said his final goodbye to her. Their loyal old Shepherd lying at her feet, refusing to leave her side...

The old man blinked back the tears in his dream as Thunder followed him down the final path. One by one, he saw them coming towards him, all the dogs of his life. He could name them all and each one brought back a different memory. He started calling out to them as they surrounded him-Sammy, how I've missed you boy! Bonnie, Barnaby, Shep, Jake and even old Sparky—the dog his family had when he was just a baby.

On and on they came, his loyal friends, how blessed he had been to have known them. He came to the end of the path with sadness, for he knew that this was where the dream would end. He had never gone past here before. He quickly scanned the horizon, hoping to catch a glimpse of just one more dog before he awoke. C'mon, he pleaded, *she* just has to be here!

He saw himself back at age six, driving into the mountains with his family. "Where are we going?" he asked for perhaps the one-hundredth time as Mom and Dad looked at each other and smiled, "You'll see!"

They drove for hours that night ending up on a curvy dirt road seemingly in the middle of nowhere. He and his sisters gasped in delight as they rounded the bend and saw a pack of golden retrievers running along in greeting. Up the long driveway, they finally stopped and he burst through the car door.

There were goldens everywhere in an outdoor enclosure, barking and huddling together with their tails wagging. He would never forget the pure joy of that day when his parents told him that this was his birthday present, a new Golden puppy. "Heavenly Goldens" the place was called and it sure was to his six-year old self. Dad picked up a curious, playful girl pup and put her in his arms. It was instant love, he thought as he remembered her light golden fur mixed with just a touch of white. As the owner of the kennel bathed her in the sink, he watched over her, impatiently waiting until he could hold her again.

Lightning. Her name was Lightning, the perfect match for Thunder the wonder Collie, he laughed, remembering the two of them together—what a pair they were! The first dog that ever belonged to him, the very best friend of his childhood years.

The old man sighed and started to go back knowing that the dream was at an end, as it had been countless of times before. In the distance, he heard a lone bark from somewhere very far away. He turned back around and saw a new path, one that had never been there before. There it was again—that bark, I know it!

All of a sudden he saw her in the distance. She began to run to him, his girl, his best friend. She leapt into his arms as he began to cry, tears of joy falling onto her light golden fur. I knew she had to be here, just knew it. He hugged her fiercely; Waggle Butt I used to call her because she would wag her entire back end whenever she saw me. Lightning licked him again, barked and headed back down the path that was now covered in mist. "Wait girl! Where are you going?"

He began to follow as she ran down the path and all of a sudden, he became that boy of six again. He could feel it, hear it in his voice. His little legs pounded the dirt path as he ran at full tilt, trying to keep up with his young golden. They rounded the next bend and he was a teenager again, strong and invincible, an invisible football clutched to his chest. Down the road they ran as boy and pup became man and dog, farther and farther as his lifetime pack of dogs followed closely behind them. She led him to a clearing, filled with endless, bright-colored wildflowers.

He stopped, old once more and vaguely made out shapes in the distance coming towards him. In the air, he could smell something cooking, a delicious aroma that evoked his childhood. He could smell the spices, expertly picking out each one and his mouth watered at the very thought of it. Such a grand meal, what flavors, what I could do with ingredients like this! I haven't really been hungry in years, he thought sadly. He had tried from time to time, but he couldn't recapture the culinary magic, hadn't been able to cook at all in recent years. His tired old body was finally giving up, fatigue and old age a losing battlefield for him. Suddenly, Lightning barked, he looked up and finally saw them.

He blinked his eyes to try to clear his sight, this can't be! His mother and father waved at him, young and smiling with joy at the sight of his gnarled, old form. His sisters were there, laughing and waving their arms as he shuffled towards them in pure wonderment. There were others here too—family, friends and old colleagues that he hadn't seen in a lifetime. Relatives he only knew from ancient picture frames beamed out at him, all beckoning him forward. In what he could only describe as a miracle, the years began to fall off again as he and Lightning crossed the prairie flowers and his true self emerged. He was young and strong again, invincible, ready to take on the world.

Another figure stepped forward and he lost all hesitation. He dashed across the field, Lightning at his heels, filled with elation and bursting with love. She fell into his arms; they were young once more, then they were old. They flickered like a light switch back and forth in their embrace, landing on how they were when they first met in Paris, nearly a century ago. If this was a dream, he thought, may I never wake up.

"No my love, this is not a dream. Lightning has brought you home and dinner is almost ready" she said as she took his hand and led him over to his family at the largest dinner table he had ever seen. All of his tools were laid out before him, his well worn knives and utensils, all of his spices and favorite ingredients prepared for him in steaming, delectable dishes. He would soon be cooking with dogs again, he thought with sudden joy. The dogs of his long life had all led him homeward to them, to her. Together again, this time for eternity.

His happiness complete, he took his place at the table next to her, with Lightning at his side and an enormous pack of dogs following behind.

The hospital room was filled to capacity. There were people everywhere, gathered around the withered old figure in the bed. His children were there, holding his hands as several generations passed by to say goodbye to their patriarch. Friends and associates stopped in to pay tribute to the Artisan, one of the greatest chefs of all time and a life well lived. They were joined in their vigil by an ancient golden retriever, his final dog, who had been given special permission by the hospital to be at his side.

Everyone had left the room, a blessed moment of silence, as she lifted her head and watched him intently. She was the only witness when he took his final breath, a smile of pure radiance on his face.

She laid her head upon his chest, a loyal friend to the very last, guarding him in his sleep.

Originally published in "Pilcrow&Dagger," May/June 2017

He Died

He died on a Friday.

The July heat was already pouring in through the weathered old screen as he perished quietly in his slumber. He'd always insisted upon the open window, even on the very coldest of nights. His wife would wrap herself in layers and layers of electric blankets in those days when they still shared the same room, time and circumstances causing them to slowly drift apart in their sleep.

Thirty-nine years as husband and wife. Decades of laughter and illness, heartbreak, and euphoria gone in the span of a single heartbeat. She would never know what did him in, only that he slept. She found him there in the first blush of morning, leaving the room before turning back and placing her hand gently on the bedroom door. The new day opened up all around her, petals on a withered flower, as she realized they would never see their fortieth year together.

He died on a Tuesday in the sweltering heat of the jungle, the bullets whizzing over his head as he crawled ass-deep through the rice paddies, muck, and shit. He was just short of his nineteenth year, one of Uncle Sam's Misguided Children traveling the world where the faint of heart would never dare to go. The explosions went off in a constant barrage, pieces of his brethren raining down all around him as he kept on going, his weapon slung over his back. He was proud and young, he was invincible. He was the favorite of the gods and therefore destined for greatness as the shrapnel from an errant grenade took him down. He was his country's greatest treasure and the source of its deepest shame. Dirty masses unleashing their spittle and scorn upon him from lofty towers, his purple heart forged in blood and brotherhood and unrequited valor.

He died on a Monday at the very moment that he saw her across the smoke-filled cocktail lounge, her long, dark hair piled high atop her head, and asked her to dance. Other men lingered like moths to a flame as he sauntered over, picked up an erstwhile beau, chair and all, and physically moved him out of his way. Her eyes were emerald green, with just a hint of blue, fathomless and pure. He felt his past shed away like a physical pain as he looked into those eyes, the spring of his life suddenly turning into summer.

He died all over again on a Thursday as they wheeled out a tiny, premature baby past him in an incubator. He placed his flask of bourbon back into his pocket as he said a silent prayer of thanks that all had gone well. He hadn't planned on a girl. It seemed impossible that this should be so, with his masculine, larger-than-life presence, yet there she was. Her scrunched up face crying down the hall convinced him that they had birthed some sort of an alien lizard, yet he loved her all the same. Fiercely and loyally, as was his nature.

On Saturday, he died as he walked her down the aisle, determined that he would walk as a man one last time, alone without oxygen or assistance of any kind. He had worked up to that goal for many months, calling upon his reserves of strength with his battered old Marine Corps handbook as a guide. On Sunday, he celebrated seeing the next generation off to their honeymoon in style, his only child launched safely into the world.

On Wednesday he died anew as his love withered and wasted away in a sterile hospital room, her memories seeping into nothingness as the brain tumor did its gruesome work. His spirit lingered on impatiently, rumbling heaven and earth in torment as he waited for her suffering to finally come to an end. She'd only been without him for eight years, had so much life yet to live, but there she was all the same. She finally joined him, placing her hand in his as they danced into eternity. Young lovers once again, twirling around and around in heavenly abandon.

He died on a Friday.

Originally published in Literally Stories, June 16, 2017 and No Extra Words Podcast, November 10, 2017

Credits

1. Chrysalis-4907
Published in Storyteller, Vol 1/Issue 1, 2017 and Bewildering Stories, 2018

2. Blood Waltz-1920
Published in Ghostlight, The Magazine of Terror, Winter/Spring 2018, Dark Fire Fiction June 2018

3. The Black Death of Happy Haven-3000
Published in Adelaide Magazine, April 2018

4. Lamentation-682
Published in Literally Stories, February 2018

5. An Appointment With Mr. Dee-2031
Published in Scrutiny Magazine, October 1, 2017

6. I'll Get By-1002
Published in Flash Fiction Magazine, March 11, 2017

7. Suspicious Minds-2566
Published in Literally Stories, December 8, 2017

8. The Cat-1507
Published in Peacock Journal, October 2016 and Write to Meow Anthology, 2018

9. Momma Said-5685
Published in Under the Bed, December 2016

10. The Boys of Little Round Top-4010
Published in Bewildering Stories, 2016

11. Furry Children-1311
Published in Friday Fiction 2016 and Dark Fire Fiction 2017

12. The Resurrectionist-1949
Published in Pilcrow&Dagger, August/September 2017 and Weird Reader 2017 Edition

13. Sourdough's Cabin-5502
Published in New Realm in 2017 and Frontier Tales in Issue #98/November 2017 (Chosen as "Reader's Choice" for November 2017)

14. Totality-1164
Published in Literally Stories, August 31, 2017

15. Terrible Beauty-5265
Published in Pilcrow&Dagger, Feb/March 2018 issue

16. The Park-994
Published in Quail Bell Magazine, March 15, 2017

17. Earworm-3275
Published in Dark Fire Fiction, December 2016

18. Family Bible-2237
Published in Edify Fiction, October 2017

19. Acceptance-2300
Published in Dark Fire Fiction, 2017

20. Bed, Bath & Way Beyond-2166
Published in Dark Fire Fiction, 2016

21. Cooking, With Dogs-5091
Published in Pilcrow&Dagger, May/June 2017

22. He Died-688
Published in Literally Stories, June 16, 2017 and No Extra Words Podcast, November 10, 2017

Acknowledgments

Many thanks to my friend Pam Engel for her patience, editing expertise and motivation when I really needed it! To Julie Trujillo, Laura Hudson, Karen Duehr, my Deja Vu sisters, and also Vickie Maybury, for helping to get the writing bug started and letting me be a part of writing sets and shows over the years. To TJ Trollinger for her help with photography and Joan Herting for designing the book cover. I also would like to acknowledge my aunt, Marilyn Kitchel, and my family and friends for your support and guidance throughout this entire journey, my love and thanks to you all!

About the Author

A. Elizabeth Herting has had short fiction stories featured in many different publications, including podcasts, reprints and poetry. She also has experience with non-fiction and as an online copywriter.

When not writing or driving kids around, she is also a member of Sweet Adelines International, a worldwide women's singing organization. She sings and competes as a Lead in a ladies barbershop quartet called Deja Vu, voted "Audience Choice/Open Division" in their regional competition for 2015, 2016 and 2018; Skyline Chorus, an International award winning group of 140 singers in Denver, Colorado; and Bella Voce, a regional first-place medaling small chorus based out of Craig, Colorado. She has been singing and performing all over the great state of Colorado (and beyond!) since 2002 and also helps to create shows and scripts as part of a writing team for those wonderful musical groups.

A. Elizabeth was proud to be selected as a Finalist in the "Adelaide Literary Award, 2018 Short Story Anthology." Her story "Sourdough's Cabin" was chosen as "Readers Choice" in the November 2017 edition of "Frontier Tales" for a future anthology. She has also had stories featured in short story anthologies: "Write to Meow," "Weird Reader 2017 Edition" and "Ghostlight, the Magazine of Terror."

A second collection of short stories called "Postcards From Waupaca" will be published by "Adelaide Books" in 2020. A. Elizabeth has also completed her first novel called "Wet Birds Don't Fly at Night" that she eventually hopes to find a home for. https://aeherting.weebly.com, twitter.com/AEHerting, facebook.com/AElizabethHerting